Meg parted Kit's thighs. Tenderly, she stroked her, then entered her. Kit moaned, her fingers pressing into Meg's shoulders. Meg continued her gentle movements, the pleasure in Kit's face building.

"Meg, I . . ." Kit's eyes were closed, her lips quivering.

"Shhh, it's okay. I love you." Kissing Kit's forehead, nose, mouth, breasts, Meg kept up the slow rhythm. In between moans Kit's breathing grew more rapid. Suddenly she stiffened, then shuddered. She emitted a soft cry and sighed deeply. Moments later, Meg stretched herself along Kit's body and, in a matched rhythm, they moved against each other. The second orgasm was shared — their fingers intertwined, their hearts beating double-time.

Afterwards, they lay quietly. Meg listened to the strong, sure thumps of Kit's pulse. Then Kit touched Meg's face, pushing her hair back along the top of her head. Fingers ran across her back. A warm breath grazed her cheek. Meg looked up and saw tears in Kit's eyes.

Family
Secrets

by

Laura DeHart Young

THE NAIAD PRESS, INC.
1996

Printed in the United States of America on acid-free paper
First Edition

Editor: Christine Cassidy
Cover designer: Bonnie Liss (Phoenix Graphics)
Typesetter: Sandi Stancil

Library of Congress Cataloging-in-Publication Data

Young, Laura DeHart, 1956 –
   Family secrets / by Laura DeHart Young.
      p.   cm.
   ISBN 1-56280-119-8 (pbk)
   1. Lesbians—Fiction. 2. Family—Fiction. I. Title.
PS3673.0799F36   1996
813'.54—dc20   95-39248
                                                  CIP

For Sue.
January 28, 1977 to forever.

Acknowledgments

Sincerest thanks to my beloved Dudley — whose snoring keeps me awake and writing.

About the Author

Laura DeHart Young's first novel, *There Will Be No Goodbyes,* was published by Naiad in 1995. She is currently at work on her third novel, *Love on the Line,* which will be published by Naiad in 1997. Laura lives with her partner of nine years in Reading, Pennsylvania. When her two pugs, Dudley and Winston, aren't demanding attention, she enjoys photography, travel and flower gardening. In her spare time, she works full-time as a writer and editor of consumer and business publications.

PROLOGUE

The sweat ran into his eyes, blurring his vision. Still he kept on running. The jungle overgrowth stung his face; mosquitoes bit and gnats covered him. Still he kept on running. Muffled shouts followed close behind, pursuing him like an animal for slaughter.

He'd tried in vain to bargain for his life. Had promised the shipment or the return of their money — plus a fifty percent penalty. He simply needed more time. The shipment was late. The money gone as a down payment. At least, that's what he'd told them. He should've known better. Never mess with these people.

They'd caught him in his hotel room as he was packing to leave the country. Trying to get out before they discovered there was no shipment — no money.

They blindfolded him and took him by car into the jungle. Into hell itself. For two days he lay in darkness on a mud floor with no food or water. When they came for him, food and water were the last things on his mind. For what were they without life? And he was about to lose his.

It was only a miracle that saved him — an attack by a rival faction. Gunfire whined through the compound. Pandemonium took hold. He escaped from the guards who were, presumably, leading him to execution.

For two nights he'd stumbled through the jungle, following the sun and stars — his natural compass. But he was on foot; they were on horseback. It hadn't been hard to find him. In his panic he'd left indelible tracks. But he kept on running, knowing where the boat was hidden. Kept doubling back and redirecting his trail toward the river. Hoping only to reach the boat in time.

He had one last plan to save his skin. One last card to play. Escape now meant a final opportunity to change the delicate balance of the game slightly in his favor. They knew where to find him. But the money and an extra shipment might make it right. Would show them he'd been true to his word. Even if he hadn't.

CHAPTER ONE

The sea wind howled, infiltrating the old house with low creaks and solemn whistles. Meg Rhyland turned over in bed, tugging the down comforter around her shoulders. She squinted at the new day coming through the corner bedroom window. The outside world was far from peaceful. With a high-pitched moan, April winds moved through the side yard and lashed the thick branches of the old oak until they almost touched the ground. Whitecaps dotted the ocean's surface like a thousand human eyes.

In the distance, resting on the higher flats, South Beach Lighthouse was clearly visible — its smooth, white tower walls and red brick base silhouetted against a turquoise sky. The clear glass prism atop the structure mirrored the sky as the lighthouse went quietly about its work, watching over eastern Nantucket Island. The lighthouse bore witness to many things known and unknown — an ocean's fury, the slow continuous passage of ships, a noisy flight of gulls, a steadily eroding shoreline.

Meg reached behind her, hand skimming across empty sheets. Kit was already up. With unaccustomed dread, she flipped the covers back. The hardwood floor was cold, its dampness shooting through her 40-year-old bones. The big house was sometimes like an unkind friend, making her feel old, exposed.

Downstairs, the aroma of coffee drifted from the kitchen. Meg shuffled groggily toward the smell and warily toward the new day.

"Hey, you're finally up."

"What time is it?"

"Nine-thirty."

"Stayed late at the shop last night."

"Coffee?"

"Please."

Meg watched as Kit reached into the cupboard for coffee mugs. The lovely, thin curving shape of Kit struck her, reminding her of the fifteen pounds she needed to lose. The blue-eyed woman with the sunset-bronze hair approached, leaning over to give Meg the mug of coffee with a morning kiss.

Quickly, Kit bounced back to the stove, rummaging for pots and pans. "Thought I'd make you breakfast. Bet you didn't eat dinner last night."

4

"No. I've got to diet anyway."

"Skipping meals is no way to diet." Opening the refrigerator, Kit grabbed a carton of eggs, bread, milk. "Finish any new pieces last night?"

"A few. Been designing a new earthenware line for the opening of the store."

"I'm proud of you, Meg. Your pottery business has really taken off."

"If things don't slow down, I'll be taking off. I need a break."

Kit cracked an egg. "The point is, you're on your way, Meg."

"Just wish I knew where I was going."

The sleek forty-two-foot yacht shone brilliant white in the sunlight. As Meg descended the salon steps to the boat's lower deck, her mind slipped back in time to a vivid image of her grandfather at the wheel of the small ship, skillfully guiding it into open water. The boat was christened *Emily* in honor of her grandmother. Her grandfather had lovingly referred to the boat as a "grand fast trawler" — though it never trawled for anything. Instead, it had been a "grand" setting for hundreds of parties and fishing trips her grandfather planned for business associates.

She remembered, not too many years ago, watching her grandfather dive from the swim platform on a muggy July afternoon. The water looked cool and refreshing. She laughed as he splashed her from beside the boat and yelled, "Meg, come in. It feels so wonderful." But she made no move to join him. The thought of jumping into the ocean terrified her. The *Emily* was her safe haven from that fear — then and now.

Today, the *Emily* belonged to Meg — along with the "big house," a stately New England seaside mansion with four floors and a view that mesmerized the stoic and romanticized even the cruelest weather. Her grandparents had been, in every sense, her parents. Even though they'd divorced just after she was born, Emily and Richard Rhyland continued a caring vigilance over her. When she was five a tragic accident changed her life forever. A car wreck killed both her parents — crushed them to death along a dark and rainy Boston street.

Meg looked around the boat's lower salon. It was the largest room on the live-aboard yacht. The dining room table was her desk, covered with papers, pens, bills and the shop's financial statements and books.

She felt disconnected with the paperwork she knew must be done — the same disconnection she'd felt the day before. She'd lied to Kit about working late. She hadn't been working. She'd been pacing — hours of tromping from one side of the room to the other. With sheer will and concentration she'd worked her memory, trying to stop the spin of her life that seemed so suddenly out of control.

Meg looked at the legal-sized envelope lying open on the table. She thumbed the edge of the envelope. The letter had arrived yesterday. Its contents concerned the estate of her grandfather who had passed away in February at the age of eighty-nine.

Meg read the bold black print: Gordon W. Meyers, Attorney at Law, Boston, Massachusetts — her grandfather's attorney. According to the brief ambiguous letter, a claim had been filed against her grandfather's estate, which was only days from being settled. The claim had been filed by a second family heir. That was the surprise, the shock, the pulling of the rug. Meg had been the only heir left in the family. Until now.

"Gordon W. Meyers, law office," the cheerful greeting was announced.

"Good morning. Meg Rhyland calling for Mister Meyers."

"One moment, please."

The boat's mobile phone crackled with white noise and static. The woman's voice returned. "Ringing Mister Meyers now, Miss Rhyland."

There was a pause, then, "Meg, Meg! Good morning. How are you?"

"Fine, Gordon. Until I received your letter."

"Make an appointment to see me, Meg. We need to discuss this claim. I'm not done looking into it yet, but it appears legitimate."

"I can be there Friday."

"Ten o'clock?"

"See you then." Meg hung up the phone with an involuntary shudder. Legitimate? Who was this person, this second heir? In the forward cabin Meg sank into the angled bed. Sunlight streamed through the small circular window, casting beams of light across murky recollections.

The past had always been fuzzy, it seemed, a kind of veil she struggled to break through. Her life sometimes felt like a dream repeating itself, continually stopping before a moment of discovery. The memories were there, somewhere just beyond her reach. The trauma of her parents' death had blocked many of them, both before and after the accident. Ironically, it was the day of the accident — that one terrible memory — she'd completely and tragically preserved.

She could see herself, a small girl sitting on a chair so large her feet dangled in the air. A familiar scent of pipe tobacco filled the room. Through the doorway, across a dimly lit corridor, the grandfather clock ticked — a sound that made the silence feel more silent. The big house frightened her when it was quiet, when there weren't any grown-ups moving through the rooms to tame it.

Suddenly, she heard footsteps up the back stairwell and a whispering sound that made her turn toward the doorway. There, her grandparents stood, the hallway light behind them making their faces dark.

"My poor little Megan," her grandfather said, stepping forward. "Sitting here in the dark all alone. Why didn't you turn on a light?"

She shifted uneasily in the uncomfortable chair, too shy to say she couldn't reach the wall switch.

"That's all right, honey. Grandpa will turn the light on."

The two big people lumbered toward the chair, kneeling down on either side. She felt squished. They looked at each other funny, then looked at her again. Had she done something bad? She tried hard to think. Something was wrong. If only she could figure out what it was.

"I'm tired. Can I go home?" She whined, hoping it would get them to say something. She'd rather have them yell at her than stare all night.

"Say, honey," her grandfather said, teeth clamping down on the stem of his pipe. "How would you like to live here for a while? With Grandpa? Near the pretty ocean."

Her grandmother put a hand on her shoulder and smiled. "You would like that, wouldn't you, Meg?"

She wouldn't. Visiting was one thing. Staying? That didn't seem right. Besides, the big house, with its nighttime creaking sounds and closed-off empty rooms, scared her. "I want to go home. Call Mommy and Daddy."

And then the world she'd known came crashing down around her with a force greater than the ocean waves she'd seen earlier that day. Her mother and father had gone to heaven. Went without her. She was going to live with her grandfather. She'd visit her grandmother on weekends in Siasconset. Her grandparents would be her new mommy and daddy. How was this possible? What mommy and daddy would leave without saying good-bye? And what about this heaven stuff? This sounded very suspicious — like made-up stories she heard in school.

Her grandfather seemed to sense her distrust, her disbelief. He tapped his pipe on the heel of his hand, his lips quivering like her own. "Megan, your parents had an accident. They didn't want to go away and leave you. They didn't know this was going to happen to them."

Now things were beginning to make more sense. An accident. A terrible thing had happened. She knew about accidents. When you fell and scraped your knee across the pavement — that was an accident. Usually, you cried. And so she did. She cried about her parents' accident ... about heaven ... about the dark old house she hated. And about the loud ticking clock outside the room that would soon be her own.

"Ahoy! Anyone home?"

Meg's mind careened to the present. Startled by the greeting from outside the upper cabin window, Meg peered through the smudged glass and saw the familiar face of her friend, Hollis Shea, mail carrier extraordinaire for the island.

"Hol, c'mon in."

"Got a package for you, kid. Special delivery." Hollis strode into the cabin, ducking her six-foot-inch frame under the doorway. She was an imposing woman — large-boned with thick muscled legs. Her daily mail route took her many miles on foot across the eastern half of the island. Parking her small vehicle along island roads, Hollis could often be seen walking narrow dirt paths, negotiating swampy bogs, pushing through high grasses and up steep bluffs, her mail bag in tow.

In spite of her size, Hollis had a sweet, lovable baby face. Her white-blonde hair was buzz-cut, sticking straight up like a freshly manicured lawn.

Hollis plopped the package on top of the two-way radio shelf, then said with a trademark grin, "Only you get personal service, Meg."

"Thanks, Hol. Saves me a trip to town. Say, where's your uniform?"

"The cleaners. Had a slight accident."

"You okay?"

"Heck, yeah. But I made an unscheduled trip into the Windswept Cranberry Bog."

"What happened?"

"Dog chased me. Big fuckin' Rottweiler." Hollis spread her arms, indicating the dog's large size. "Broke away from its owner — an old granny no less than ninety. Damned dog chased me all the way down Polpis Road. It was catchin' up quick so I ran into the bog."

"Did it follow you?"

"Nope. Didn't like the idea of gettin' its feet wet. Course, that's what I'd hoped. So there I am, up to my knees in cranberries. I start wavin' my arms — shooin' the dog away, but it won't budge. Just stands there at the edge, barkin' its fool head off. So I take a step forward, clap my hands and yell real loud. Then, my boot gets sucked into the mud at the bottom of the bog. Now I'm standin' on one foot yellin' and wavin' my arms. Next thing you know, a big gust of wind hits, knockin' me flat on my ass."

Meg put her hand to her mouth, stifling a laugh.

"Oh, it's funny now," Hollis said, chuckling loudly. "But it wasn't so funny then. When I got up outta that bog, I saw the contents of my mail bag spread near and far. There were letters stuck up in the trees."

Hands wrapped around her sides, Meg shook with laughter. Tears were running down her cheeks. The thought of the big woman lying flat in the bog was too much.

"Do you know, I was pickin' old and rotten cranberries from my hair all day long?" Hollis frowned. "Never did get my boot back."

"Well, you know what they say, Hol."

"Yeah, yeah. The damned mail must go through."

"Preferably not through the bog."

"You got that right." Clasping her hands behind her back, Hollis sauntered over to the instrument panel. "You still usin' the boat as your office?"

"Yeah, it's peaceful here. And I can take off into the great blue whenever I want."

"How're things with Kit? She owns part of the restaurant now, I heard."

"Amazing, isn't it?" Kit had bought a share in The Back Alley Tavern in Provincetown where she worked as the manager. "She's happy. We're happy."

"What's it been now, three, four years?"

"Over four years."

"Ah, yes. Christmas. And to think that I introduced you two. But if she ever gets sick of you, let me know." Hollis winked, picking up the two-way radio mike. "Now hear this. Beautiful woman looking for same to share quiet moments."

Meg laughed. "C'mon, Hol. The women are beating down your door."

"Ha! You know all my secrets. Say, did I tell you about the pretty babe I saw the other night?" Hollis splayed her hands in front of her chest. "Nice big ones. I think she liked me too. Bought her a few drinks and she hung around for a while. Got her phone number." Hollis flashed a piece of paper with some numbers scribbled on it.

"Hol, you've always been a hit with the women. What's your secret, anyway?"

"Charm, kid. Total charm. Guess you have it or you don't. Well, I'll be movin' along. You still owe me another ride on this old tub."

"I'll call you in a few weeks. We'll have a picnic on the water."

"No kiddin'?"

"No kidding. It's time to clear out the winter cobwebs."

The afternoon light faded slowly across the small strip of sand below the big house. Meg walked toward home, her arms clasped across her chest to break the wind. Hers was a way of life she'd grown to love, she thought. Even the endless ocean she'd feared since childhood was sometimes a friend. At night, the rhythmic rolling of waves lulled her to sleep. In the morning, deep blue-green reflections welcomed her to a new day. During afternoon walks, the wind from over the water moved gently through her hair — the salty smell refreshing, invigorating.

She couldn't believe it might be taken away from her. A recent letter and phone call had brought her face-to-face with that threat. Looking up toward the big house, Meg saw everything she had left of her family — not so much the wood, stone, steel and glass that shaped the massive structure, but the collective essence of it speaking to her of where she'd been and who she'd become. It was a place that had held her safe from not knowing; where big surprises came but were conquered, where she expected to die, playing out the final scene like in an old Hollywood movie, shaking her fist at the raging ocean.

Every grain of sand, every gnarled tree was in her blood. It was the house where she'd last seen her parent's alive, where trees and flower gardens were nurtured from the soil by her grandmother, where as a child she'd stalked evil pirates whose great ships rose suddenly above the horizon. Not far away, a boat named *Emily* rocked gently in its slip. She'd become rooted to the place like the old oak before her, bent toward the house by wind and will.

From behind, two arms suddenly enveloped her. "You're home early."

Meg turned to find Kit's eyes — soft, familiar, delicately blue. "Needed a break."

"Missed you today." Slowly, Kit's hands moved underneath Meg's jacket and shirt, gently caressing her breasts. "Why don't we go inside?"

"What time must you be at the restaurant?"

Kit kissed her, a warm tongue skimming along her own. In between breaths she whispered, "I did morning duty. Tom's supervising the renovations this afternoon. Don't have to go in till seven."

Meg glanced at her watch. "That's a whole four hours from now."

"Deduct forty-five minutes for the ferry and another twenty minutes to Provincetown."

"Let's go inside."

Canopies of gray afternoon light kept darkness from the room, leaving the corners in shadow.

Reaching out, Meg stroked Kit's face and looked into eyes that told again of gentleness and shyness — vulnerabilities known only to Meg. Meg smiled at the serious face, at the familiar touch of a hand along her thigh. Lips parted, hot with a kiss.

Their love-making had evolved slowly, Kit's shyness apparent from their very first night together. The big house had been decorated festively for the holidays and for the party Meg had decided to give. A large pine cone wreath was draped over the stone fireplace. Bayberry candles scented the dining room. In the living room, an eight-foot blue spruce was covered from trunk to tip with popcorn and cranberry strands, tiny twinkling lights and handmade ornaments.

Nearby, Meg's grandfather sat in a rocker tending the fire, stoking the flames with one hand, lighting his pipe with the other. Around his neck, tucked into a gray flannel shirt, was the red scarf Meg had given him for Christmas.

"These ladies you've invited. Do I know any of them?" he asked, his ruddy complexion illuminated by the hearth.

"I think you've met a few, Papa. And anyway, I don't remember your having an aversion to meeting new women."

"Never." He smiled, talking around the pipe stem. "You never get too old for that."

Meg leaned over and kissed the old man. His rough face scratched her cheek. "Papa, you need a shave."

"Do I?" He rubbed his chin. "By God, you're right. Must've forgotten this morning."

"There's still time — an hour or so."

"Well, I'll put some more wood on this fire and then fix myself up a bit."

Two hours later, Richard Rhyland had danced with almost every woman in the house.

"Meg, Hollis and I are going to elope. Then we're taking a cruise to the Bahamas," her grandfather announced. His thin silver hair fell across his forehead as he bent to kiss Hollis's hand.

"Hol, are you trying to pick up Papa?"

"Listen, I'd marry him in a second. He wouldn't make me lug that damned mail bag all over the island. I'd be wined and dined. Treated like a queen."

"I don't know, Hol. Sometimes this guy can be a handful."

Richard Rhyland bowed at the waist. "Nonsense. I'm not a handful. I'm one of the last true gentlemen left, the kind of man who knows how a lady likes to be treated. But it *is* past my bedtime. So, goodnight ladies. Don't stay up too late." He said good night to everyone, then shuffled slowly up the steps.

"What a great guy, Meg." Hollis smiled.

"Yeah, he's very special." And not a bad dancer, either, she thought.

In one continuous breath, Hollis said, "Hey, Meg, want you to meet someone — friend of mine — just got here a few minutes ago. Had to work late."

Before Meg could object, Hollis had grabbed her by the arm and dragged her toward the kitchen where a loud, though small group of women had congregated. Hollis was always introducing her to women. How she managed to meet these dozens of lovely ladies Meg had yet to discover. Silently, she vowed to find out. Hollis steered Meg toward a lone woman who stood sipping a drink, her eyes politely intent on the raucous antics of the women nearby.

Of medium height and build with long auburn hair bunching in waves along her shoulders, she wore tight-fitting blue jeans that hugged the small sleek curves of her hips. Her face was serious and intense — cream-colored skin crinkling slightly at the mouth. Staring out from that stunning face were piercing baby-blue eyes.

"Kit," Hollis called.

At the sound of her name the woman looked up, flashing a half-smile.

"This is Meg Rhyland, our host for the evening," Hollis said, still clutching Meg's forearm. "Meg, this is Kit Stone. She manages The Back Alley Tavern in Provincetown."

Meg held out her hand. "Nice to meet you. Glad you could join us tonight." Feeling a sudden connection as Kit's eyes met her own, Meg thought she heard herself gasp.

Kit took Meg's hand, smiling weakly. Softly she said, "Hello."

Meg's head felt hollow, the words echoing from one empty side to the other. "Hope you're enjoying the party." Awkwardly, Meg realized she was still holding Kit's hand. With reluctance, she let go.

"Your house is lovely, Meg." Kit cocked her head toward the sliding glass doors in the next room. "Must be beautiful on a clear day."

"Come back when the sun is shining."

Kit hesitated, clearing her throat. "Thanks. I will."

"Never been to your restaurant. I'll have to make up for that oversight."

"I'll see that you get a good table."

"And if you get a chance, stop by my store. The Pottery Kiln, downtown Nantucket."

Three days later, Meg nervously dialed the number for The Back Alley Tavern. She paced back and forth, listening to restaurant sounds at the other end as someone went to fetch Kit Stone. Mouth like cotton, palms sweating, she tried to stop her heart from racing.

"Kit Stone."

"Kit, Meg Rhyland. We met last weekend at my house."

"Oh, hi . . ." The voice faltered.

"I'd like to make reservations at your restaurant."

"Great. How many people?"

"Two."

"What night?"

"What night do you have off?"

"Excuse me?"

"What night are you free?"

"Uh, Friday."

"Then I'd like to make the reservations for Friday. I thought you might have dinner with me." Silence. "I guess I'm asking you for a date. But it's been a while, so if I'm screwing it up, I'm sorry."

"No. I'd like that. What time?"

"What time do you finish work tonight?"

"Eleven."

"Want to have a drink?"

"Sure."

"I'll pick you up at the restaurant."

Meg parked in front of the restaurant and waited. Following the phone call with Kit, a delightful high had taken control of her mind — one that no drug could duplicate. Excitement. Anticipation. Hysteria. All the emotions necessary to concoct a thrill not offered by any amusement park ride. Meeting someone. It was like falling off a cliff in slow motion and ever hitting the ground. Meg hadn't experienced those feelings in a long time. She wasn't quite sure what to do with them. Then Kit emerged from the restaurant, opened the car door and slid in next to her. Life, she thought, was sometimes very sweet. She'd try to enjoy the feelings for as long as possible.

For four months they dated — dinner, drinks, dancing. They went to the movies, shopped, held hands along the beach front. They'd kissed a few times, but Kit was so overtly nervous that Meg didn't push it.

One evening, she invited Kit to see the *Emily*.

"Want to take a ferry boat ride tonight?" she asked. "You haven't seen the *Emily* yet. It's quiet there. We can just relax and talk."

Kit agreed, looking particularly anxious, then managed a smile, quickly replaced by a meek seriousness Meg would grow to recognize. "Before I met you, Meg, my life was work. Not much more. I never thought about anyone being interested in me."

"Why? You're a terrific person."

Kit shrugged. "I haven't had much experience dating or anything. I've..."

"What?"

She looked directly into Meg's eyes. "I'm thirty years old, and I've never been with anyone. I mean, sexually."

"And you don't have to be with anyone now if you don't want to."

"That's just it, Meg. I do."

Meg walked from the boat's main salon down the steps into the adjoining galley. "Would you like a beer, or something stronger?"

A quiet voice replied, "Stronger. Scotch and water if you have it. With ice, please."

"You're in luck. Papa always keeps a bottle on board." Drinks in hand, Meg went back into the salon, almost tripping over the single step in front of her. Kit wasn't the only one who was nervous, she thought.

Sitting down on the couch, Kit reached for the glass. "Thanks."

"Welcome."

Kit took in the room with one concentrated gaze. "You work here when you're not at the shop?"

"Yes. Pay bills, keep track of inventory, that kind of thing. Not my favorite part of the business."

"What's your favorite part?"

"Meeting people."

"Are you glad you met me?"

"Extremely."

From the turned-down bed Meg watched steam from the recently used shower escape into the room. Kit had just emerged clutching a borrowed flannel robe around her — her face, hair and skin still damp. Meg's clothes already lay in a heap on the bathroom floor. She got up from the bed and stood in front of Kit, her mind skipping over thoughts like a scratched record. Unable to focus on any single emotion, she smiled and put her hands on Kit's waist. As Meg kissed her Kit trembled in her arms. Then Meg untied the bathrobe, slipping it from Kit's shoulders, letting it fall to the floor.

Between the sheets Kit curled into a ball at the edge of the bed, her back toward Meg. Meg kissed her neck, shoulders, arms. "It's okay, Kit. We can just talk if you want."

Kit turned over. "Will you hold me?"

"Of course." Meg put her arms around Kit's shoulders and took a deep breath. "I love you, Kit." It was the first time she'd said it.

"I love you too."

Meg kissed her, then ran her tongue down Kit's neck to her chest. Kit's breasts were lovely, sensuous. She followed the soft skin to a nipple. In her mouth she could feel Kit's excitement, the nipple suddenly hard. Kit sighed and ran her fingers through Meg's hair, tracing the outline of her ears.

"Meg . . ."

Meg looked up. Kit was smiling.

"Kiss me again."

Meg kissed Kit's chin, nibbled the edges of her lips, deepened the kiss.

Kit laughed nervously, running her tongue along Meg's neck. "I think if you touch me, I'll explode."

Meg whispered, "Really? Let's find out."

Meg parted Kit's thighs. Tenderly, she stroked her, then entered her. Kit moaned, her fingers pressing into Meg's shoulders. Meg continued her gentle movements, the pleasure in Kit's face building.

"Meg, I . . ." Kit's eyes were closed, her lips quivering.

"Shhh, it's okay. I love you." Kissing Kit's forehead, nose, mouth, breasts, Meg kept up the slow rhythm. In between moans Kit's breathing grew more rapid. Suddenly she stiffened, then shuddered. She emitted a soft cry and sighed deeply. Moments later, Meg stretched herself along Kit's body and, in a matched rhythm, they moved against each other. The second orgasm was shared — their fingers intertwined, their hearts beating double-time.

Afterwards, they lay quietly. Meg listened to the strong, sure thumps of Kit's pulse. Then Kit touched Meg's face, pushing her hair back along the top of her head. Fingers ran across her back. A warm breath grazed her cheek. Meg looked up and saw tears in Kit's eyes.

Meg shook herself back to the present. Memories rushed like a fast forwarding movie . . . blurred images, garbled voices. Meg loved this woman with as much passion as she had four years earlier. Curled into each other's arms, Meg heard the same excitement breathing in the shadows. It hadn't faded over the years.

Kit exhaled a long hard breath. A hand grasped Meg's arm, pulling her upward. Here were the eyes, that shade of sterling blue peaceful, satisfied. Kit. Meg repeated the name to herself until finally she said it aloud.

"What?"

"Nothing. Just wanted to say your name."

Kit kissed Meg's cheek, then lay her head on the pillow, smiling so that her nose crinkled. "You make me want to stay all night. But I have to go now."

"You may go. So long as you always come back."

"Not much could keep me away."

CHAPTER TWO

The Boston Hilton was bustling as Meg sat in the lobby reading a day-old newspaper. Suddenly, she felt two hands squeeze her shoulders from behind. There was a kiss on her temple and a whispered, "Hey, beautiful. Your date's here."

Meg leapt out of the chair. "Brad! No fair sneaking up on me like that!"

"Sorry, sweetie. God, I've missed you!"

Meg took two steps backward, looking at the tall slim Brad Hanson, her old "boy next door." For five years they lived on the same block, and from junior high on they'd been inseparable. The fact that they were both from broken homes solidified their friendship. His parents were divorced, her parents were dead and grandparents divorced. Brad was her strength, her first crush, the first and only boy she ever kissed. Then the war came. Brad was drafted and sent to Vietnam. For three hundred and sixty-five days Meg lived in terror that he wouldn't return. When he extended his tour of duty until the end of the war she withdrew into herself, unforgiving of him and suddenly confused about everything.

While he was away Meg started college. During her freshman year at Emerson, she met a woman, a graduate student pursuing a masters degree in communications. They fell in love and started a serious relationship. She pulled herself from Brad's shadow into the light of a beautiful woman's arms — where she stayed for the next three years. When Brad finally returned at the war's end, there was an initial awkward confrontation. Eventually, they came to understand each other. He loved the military. She loved women. In spite of this great chasm they had vowed to remain friends and saw each other at least once a month, depending on his schedule.

Meg stared at the handsome businessman in front of her, his curly blond hair and boyish grin a welcome sight. He looked terrific — skin darkened by a recent vacation to the Bahamas. A professional appraiser and estate auctioneer, he traveled all over the world. It was hard to believe. She still remembered the boy who carried her books to school, gave her a first kiss, took her to the high school prom.

"What's the matter, Meg? Do I look that bad?"

"You look great. I was thinking about the old days."

Brad hooked his arm through hers. "Follow me. We can talk about the old days over lunch."

They found a nearby restaurant and during their meal a nostalgic conversation swung to the present. After hearing about Meg's legal problems, concern replaced Brad's vibrant smile.

"When's the meeting with Meyers, Meg?"

"Tomorrow."

Brad pushed his half-eaten bowl of soup away and leaned back in his chair. His squared jaw was set, his eyes lost somewhere in thought. After a minute or two of silence he tried to reassure her. "Meyers has been my attorney for fifteen years. He's thorough and knows his stuff. Even more, he knows your family's legal history. If there're any problems with the legitimacy of this claim, Gordon'll find out."

"Thanks. That's all I needed to hear. I feel better already."

He squeezed her hand. "Tell me about your store in Provincetown. What great news."

"Yes, I'm finally opening the second shop."

"I'm proud of you, Meg." He looked up from his salad, his eyes beaming. "How's Kit?"

"Good. Come to dinner at the big house. She'll love seeing you again."

"I'll be in town for two weeks. Then it's back to Europe. I'm handling some big estate auctions in Paris and London."

"Sounds exciting."

"The travel gets old, but I enjoy meeting people. Keeps the job interesting. My clients are mostly wealthy jet-setters. I suppose there are some advantages to rubbing shoulders with the rich."

"I can only imagine."

"But the best part's coming home. There's something about the island that keeps calling me back. You're part of that, Meg."

"I'm glad." She smiled, happy to see him, relieved that Gordon Meyers was her lawyer.

Kit threw her jacket across the kitchen chair. She was agitated, excited. And slightly drunk. "Not one damned thing's gone right, Meg. I don't know what to do."

"The restaurant?"

"Everything's a mess. The contractors are behind schedule. The reopening is only a few weeks away. The chef is being temperamental about the new menu. And everybody's tired and bitchy."

"So I see."

Ice cubes clinked into a glass of straight scotch. "I should just sell my interest in that damned place. It's not worth the trouble." Kit sank into a chair and took a healthy gulp of her drink.

"Things'll come together. Try not to worry."

"I've got a lot of money tied up in the success of this, Meg. Everything's got to be perfect. It was all my idea. To close the restaurant, renovate and reopen. If it's a disaster, it's my disaster."

Meg got up, put her arms around Kit's shoulders. "You're being very hard on yourself. I'm having some problems with the new shop too. It's bound to happen. Just keep focused and everything will fall into place. You're the best at what you do. It's going to be a smashing success."

"Think so?"

"Absolutely."

Kit sighed heavily. "There's so much work to be done . . ."

"Then you better get some rest. You don't need a hangover on top of everything else."

"You go ahead. I'll be up soon."

An hour later, staring at the darkness, Meg was still alone and concerned. Mentally keeping pace with Kit, who sat downstairs worrying. And drinking.

Inside the beige-walled office with its walnut wainscoting and leather furniture, Meg sat impatiently chewing on her bottom lip. A view of the Boston skyline, visible through an expansive picture window, was the only interesting distraction. A hum of voices filtered into the room from the outer hallway, matching the hum of thoughts in her head. Thoughts she would rather not deal with on this or any other day.

The office door behind her opened. She felt a rush of air, sensed movement in the room as a vibration of muffled footsteps hurried across the carpeted floor.

Gordon Meyers extended his hand with a lawyer-like smile she considered invasive. "Meg, great to see you. How was the trip up?"

Dressed impeccably in a dark blue suit Gordon positioned the leather chair closer to the desk, then flopped himself down. A whoosh of air was expelled from the cushion beneath him. The man appeared to be in his early sixties. That would be about right, Meg thought. He'd graduated from Boston College the same year as her father.

She looked up, remembering his question about her trip to Boston. "Uneventful."

"Good. How's business?"

Meg feigned a smile. Small talk. A necessary evil. "Fine, Gordon."

He grinned, but Meg could tell he was nervous; his forehead was perspiring. From underneath a stack of papers, he produced a file about three inches thick. "Meg, you know that my own father was your grandfather's attorney for many years before he died and I took over the firm. I continued to represent your grandfather in all his legal affairs until he retired and liquidated many of his business holdings." Gordon stopped, scratched his nose and cleared his throat. "His goals were always simple — to make certain that his assets, including a long-established trust fund, went to his heirs and this included your grandmother, before she died. Until recently, it all seemed elementary. You were his only heir."

"Correct."

"According to your grandfather's will, which you and I already reviewed some weeks ago, all of his wishes were complied with. Until now."

"You said there was another claim filed against the estate." Meg was trying to keep her voice down.

Gordon collapsed backward into his chair. The overhead lights reflected onto a scalp almost totally vacant of hair. Five or six remaining clumps had been combed in strands across the front of his head, a failed attempt to disguise reality. Other than the unfortunate baldness, Meyers seemed to be in excellent condition for a man his age. His physique was trim, neck thick and muscular.

"Right. After the claim was filed I did some more research. To my utter surprise I found a misfiled document — a legal codicil to his will. It'd been prepared almost fifteen years ago by my father." He leaned forward again, opening the file folder and removing several legal-sized forms. "The codicil consists of two pages meant to be a supplement to the original will your grandfather also prepared with the help of this office. It names another heir to share equally in the settlement of the estate."

"Who?" Meg held her breath.

"The individual's name is Michael Shaun Gregory — your father's son, your half-brother."

Sitting in stunned silence, Meg forced herself to breathe. Half-brother? Father's son? A cruel joke. Some kind of hoax. "This is absurd. I don't have a brother. My father never had a son. I'm afraid there's been a mistake."

"No mistake, Meg. I'm sorry to tell you this." Gordon removed a handkerchief from his pants pocket and dabbed his forehead. "Your father had an affair with a woman named Sheila Gregory. She worked as a receptionist in his surgical office from nineteen fifty-six to nineteen sixty. Miss Gregory became pregnant toward the end of the affair. Your father refused to recognize the child as his own. But your grandfather felt differently."

"Meaning?"

"Richard Rhyland was a fair and honest man, Meg. I'm sure you know that."

"Of course."

"As I understand it, your father and grandfather argued bitterly over Michael's legitimacy in the family. Sheila Gregory came to your grandfather for help. She claimed she wanted nothing for herself. Her only concern was for her son's future. Your grandfather refused to get legally involved until after your father's death. The thought of the young boy haunted him for almost twenty years before he took action." He handed her a letter dated March 28, 1980. "Until nineteen eighty to be exact. That's when he made Michael an heir."

Meg scanned the letter signed by her grandfather. It corroborated everything Meyers had just told her. "I can't believe Papa would keep this from me. How could he?"

Gordon shrugged helplessly. "I can't answer that, Meg. You have to understand that I also was unaware of this until the papers were brought to my attention last week. The codicil somehow became separated from the original will and, as surprising as it may sound, your grandfather never discussed it with me."

"Have you talked to Michael Gregory?"

"Yes. He lives on Martha's Vineyard."

Meg fought for composure. "Is there any way we can challenge this? Any loopholes?"

"I'm afraid not. Mister Gregory has a legal legitimate right to half your grandfather's estate."

Meg got up from her chair. She felt woozy. "What are you telling me, Gordon? That I'm going to lose half of everything?"

"I've asked for a meeting with Mister Gregory. He wants to view the property and go over the estate's assets so a fair settlement can be reached. I suggest we comply with this request."

Meg leaned over Meyers' desk, her hands clenched into white fists. She shook her head slowly, meeting Gordon's eyes. "I must be dreaming, Gordon. It can't be."

"I'll arrange a meeting and call you next week, Meg. I'm sorry."

"One last question. How do we know this Michael Gregory person is really my father's son by this woman — Sheila Gregory?"

"Your grandfather hired a private detective in nineteen eighty to investigate the matter. My father recommended that he do so. The evidence, though not conclusive, supported Sheila Gregory's claims."

Meg straightened, stepping away from Gordon's desk, suddenly embarrassed by her show of emotion. "Please send me copies of that report along with the complete file on my grandfather's estate. I'll need to do some homework before meeting my long lost half-brother."

Gordon stepped from behind his desk. "Now, Meg, that's what you're paying me for. I've gone through everything quite thoroughly. There's no need for you to be mired down in paperwork."

"I want to be fully informed before I sit down with anyone claiming half-ownership of my family's estate. And that means looking at every piece of paper myself."

"If you insist. I'll have a courier stop by the house."

"Thank you." Meg headed toward the door. She was trembling.

"By the way, you needn't worry about the *Emily*," Meyers called after her. "In both your grandfather's will and the codicil the boat was left specifically to you."

Meg turned back toward Gordon. "Thank you. I'll sleep so much better now — knowing I'll at least have some place to live."

Pulling into the driveway, Meg looked up at the big house with a sense of impending doom. The entire trip back she'd searched her memory, trying to recall something, anything that would have hinted of her family's well-kept secret. But she'd been so young then that nothing except faint voices and distorted images registered now.

The heavy front door of the big house opened to the smell of vanilla candles. Meg walked into the dining room freshly scented with lemon wax. She dropped her coat and briefcase on the Boston rocker and went through the hallway to the kitchen where Kit, a wooden spoon in one hand, scotch glass in the other, was stirring the contents of a sizable pot. She was dressed in gray sweatpants and a navy blue thermal shirt tightly outlining her lovely curving breasts. Meg smiled. Kit was a welcome sight. Steam rose, masking her face.

"What's cooking?" Meg asked.

"Dinner. Thought you'd be tired. I'm making my famous stew."

"My favorite."

Kit motioned her into the room. "Have a taste."

After blowing lightly on the steaming broth, Kit held the spoon to Meg's lips. "What do you think? Need anything?"

"No. Perfect." Meg watched Kit finish her drink, then watched her make another.

"Can I fix you a scotch, hon?"

"Little early for that, don't you think?"

Kit shrugged. "It's Friday. I'm off tonight. So, why not?"

"We need to talk, Kit. I have news."

Kit approached her, softly kissing her forehead just above the bridge of her nose. "You look worried."

"The mystery of my life has suddenly taken a decidedly different turn."

Water lapped the boat as the craft drifted to a stop just beyond Great Point. Meg lowered the anchor into the calm water. Mid-May had been sunny and surprisingly warm — mild and windless. This day was no different, perfect for a cruise into the great blue.

Across the starboard deck, Kit arranged a picnic lunch. Steamed shrimp and clams, fruit salad, cheese and crackers, raw vegetables and dip, chilled white wine and beer was the menu for the afternoon. A large quilted blanket substituted for a table. Four low, sea-green beach chairs hugged its perimeter.

Two glasses and wine bottle in hand, Kit strolled

across the deck, her light gauze dress flapping in the wind. "Lunch is ready."

"Where are the other two crew members?"

Kit placed a glass in Meg's hand and filled it. "Touring the boat."

"Mmmm. Not sure we should let Hol give a tour. She's liable to include the bedrooms and we may never see them again."

Kit giggled. "Well, at any rate, it gives us time for a toast."

"What're we toasting?"

Kit smiled, stroking her chin thoughtfully. "Oh, let me think." Leaning forward, she kissed Meg lightly on the lips. "Here's to my lover. To our life together. To great sex — long winter nights and steamy summer days."

Outwardly, Meg grinned. Inside, she worried. Bold comments for Kit to make. "No problem drinking to those things," Meg responded, looking into Kit's large glistening eyes. As always, they were magnificently blue and, today, slightly bloodshot. A few too many drinks already.

"And something else, too."

"Name it."

"To getting through these next few months on the strength we've always given each other."

"I've got a feeling we're going to need it."

"Hey, you two. Is it soup yet?"

Kit swung around, using her hand to shield the sun from her eyes. "Take it easy, Hollis. You won't starve."

"Unless she's been working up an appetite below."
Hollis's eyes brightened. "Hmmm, not a bad idea.
But I'm hungry enough right now." The large woman
took Meg by the arm. "C'mon, Meg. And bring the
cook with you."

Meg sat next to Hollis. Directly across from her,
Hollis's friend, Cass, chatted with Kit as they helped
themselves to lunch. Cass was all legs — long shapely
limbs stretching out from an even shapelier body.
Straight waist-length hair, jet black, fell in layers
down her back. Meg remembered seeing her a few
months before, dancing seductively with a group of
women in a Provincetown club.

"Meg, Cass is a singer." Kit slid the last available
chair away from direct sunlight, stumbling into it
with an unflattering bounce. "She plays with a band
called Tidalwave at the Jade Hourglass in
Provincetown. We were there once. Bradford Street.
Remember?"

"I think so."

Cass smiled, stretching her long legs forward.
"Hope you don't mind, Meg, but I told Kit to zip on
by some night next week. She likes jazz and our
band's opening with a new gig on Tuesday. It'll be a
hoot."

Meg nodded. "I'm sure."

"Cass and I met at The Breaker," Hollis said. "I
was sittin' at the bar. Accidentally dropped a
ten-dollar bill on the floor. Bent down to pick it up
and all I saw were these two gorgeous legs. Shoulda
dropped a fifty. God knows what I woulda saw."

Cass's eyelids fluttered, her lips pursed around a wedge of melon. "Hollis, honey, I'm worth more than a fifty, aren't I?"

Hollis opened a beer, foam flying in all directions. "Hey, I've gotta pass out hundred-dollar bills to keep the other ladies away from you." Sipping the oozing foam, Hollis turned to Kit with a grin. "Kit, you been shakin' these beer cans, or what?"

Kit scowled, a drop of wine slipping down her chin. "Yes, just to annoy you, Hollis! No, I haven't been shaking the beer cans. I merely removed them from the refrigerator!"

Hollis put up her hands. "Okay, okay. I was only kiddin'."

"Don't know how you can drink that stuff anyway." Kit struggled to her feet. "I'm going to make myself a scotch. Anybody else want one?"

Cass got up, smoothing out the wrinkles in her tight leather pants. "I'll have one, Kit. Besides, I'd like to see that adorable little kitchen again. Mind if I come along?"

"Not at all."

"The galley," Meg called after them.

"What?" Cass asked with a quizzical expression.

Meg sighed. "On a boat the kitchen's called a galley."

The long-legged woman bobbed her head, giggling softly. "Oh, how cute."

Meg watched the two women disappear below. The wine was beginning to take effect, bringing a soothing numbness to irritating thoughts.

Hollis leaned forward, waving her hand in front of Meg's face. "Still here?"

"Yep."

"What's with Kit? Seems a little edgy."

"Don't know. The restaurant, I guess."

"And this legal mess of yours? Really think you'll lose the house?"

"Not without a fight. I'm not going to let some stranger take it away, no matter who he says he is."

"Think this guy's really your brother?"

"I don't know, Hol. My childhood is such a blank I'm not sure of anything. The only thing I remember with absolute clarity is the day my parents were killed. Everything else is foggy. Bits and pieces. Don't you think that's strange?"

"I can hardly remember what I did yesterday, Meg. And let's not forget, you're forty now."

Meg frowned. "Thanks for reminding me. You know, it's suddenly occurred to me — I'm not sure I really knew my grandfather all that well."

"Why do you say that?"

"Hell, he was always gone. Business trips. Working late. He was a sweet old man and I loved him. But he was tight-lipped." Meg laughed. "Oh, he used to tell me stories about World War Two — fighting the Japanese in India. Stuff like that. But not how he felt about things." Meg took another sip of wine. "He mellowed in his later years. Not so silent. We were closer then — when it was too late."

"Guess you can't say the same about us."

"No, Hol. And I'm glad."

"Remember when we first met?"

Meg chuckled. "Do I ever! You tried to pick me up at that bar downtown."

"Yeah. I did, didn't I?" Hollis slapped her knee. "God, we were young dykes then."

"And crazy."

"Hey, Meg. This lawyer of yours — Meyers. He any good?"

"Between Gordon Meyers and his father they've been representing my family for almost sixty years. I'd like to believe he knows what he's doing."

"You know, maybe you should get a second opinion. See what another lawyer says." Hollis crushed her empty beer can. "Or you could hire a private investigator."

Surprised, Meg looked at her. "Private investigator? I don't need one of those. Besides, it would cost a lot of money. I need every penny now. Especially if I've got to buy half the house back from this Gregory guy. And I've got the new shop opening in July."

"Thought your grandfather set up a trust fund for you."

"I may lose half of that too."

"Well, give the private investigator thing some thought. There's a lot at stake, Meg." Hollis stood up and they went below. Laughter could be heard from the galley where Kit and Cass were drinking scotch and swapping stories.

"Sounds like they're having fun, Hol. Maybe we've been out in the sun too long."

"You know, this really pisses me off. I think my date's after your woman."

Meg laughed. "Don't be ridiculous."

"I'm serious, Meg. Cass practically undressed Kit with her eyes. Being the pro that I am I don't miss much of this stuff."

"You and your dates, Hol. Maybe if you'd concentrate on one lovely lady for more than a few days these things wouldn't happen."

"Yeah, and then I'd have no fun. But I'm tellin' you, friend. Cass is after your wife. You should listen to me. Your powers of observation have never been that good."

"Well, if what you think's true I'm not worried. Kit and I are solid. In fact, except for you, Kit's the only solid thing I have left in my life." Meg looked at Hollis, then back toward the galley. "I hope."

The electrically powered wheel, spinning and whirring, had the power to mesmerize. Meg could feel the textured clay, soft and wet against her hands, being shaped from an image that existed only inside her head. Eventually, it would unfold before her. It was always that way — each piece a surprise, an adventure.

"Meg, the new earthenware's packed. Linda'll pick it up in an hour or so. Any other pieces to go?"

The wheel stopped, the image in her mind suddenly blank and formless, yet still there, waiting. Meg spun in the stool, her eyes readjusting from the blur of the wheel to the rigidity of the room. Carl was standing in the doorway, his muscular form the result of a daily five-mile run. Both Carl and his wife, Linda, worked for Meg. Like Meg, Carl was a potter, specializing in salt-glazed stoneware. Linda was Meg's administrative right arm and the manager of the new store in Provincetown.

"Sorry. Shouldn't bother you while you're working."

Meg felt her presence drift back into the room. "I was a million miles away."

Carl smiled. Dressed in a gray smock over a navy sweater and jeans, he glanced into the boxes stacked on the floor nearby. "Linda'll be here soon to transport more inventory. The earthenware's packed. Anything else?"

"You can use those boxes to pack the pieces I finished last night. On the shelf over there."

Carl approached the shelf where several vases, lamp bases, pitchers and bowls rested. "I see you used the new glazes. Beautiful."

"The alkaline glazes, yes. But I added a touch more sand and biscuit-fired the pieces first. The iron additive produced that vibrant blue. I've never seen it before. What do you think?"

"They'll sell out the first day."

"Hope you're right." Meg turned and stared at the wheelhead. Sitting there was the half-finished piece she no longer recognized. "Sometimes I wonder where this stuff comes from and when it's going to stop."

"Sounds like you need a break. I brought lunch."

"Great. Let's go down to the ferry stop."

At the edge of the parking lot near the Nantucket Ferry stop, Meg and Carl ate lunch while staring out over the white-blue water. To their left tourists wandered by, filtering along the streets in small numbers that would soon swell to hundreds, then thousands. Meg could feel the oncoming rush. The onslaught. The furor of another season.

"Get the papers from your lawyer?" Carl asked between bites of his sandwich.

"Should've had them two weeks ago. But I'm expecting them any day."

Carl squeezed Meg's arm. She could feel the warm pressure of his hand, strong and comforting. "This whole mess'll get straightened out. I know it will." Carl shifted toward Meg, leaning back against a piling. "How're things with Kit?"

"Strained. I'm worried about her drinking, Carl. It's getting worse. I mean, she's always been a drinker, but this is different."

"How so?"

"It's not just once or twice on the weekends anymore. It's before dinner, after dinner. At the restaurant."

Carl brushed some grass from his khakis, his muscled thighs visible through the fabric. "Maybe Kit's worried about your legal problems too. She might be more upset than you think. Could be her way of dealing with the stress."

Meg turned. Carl's platinum-blond hair had been taken by the wind — matted against the brown piling like soft, white-gold netting. "You may be right. But I need Kit's support more than ever. And she seems to really need the drinking."

"I've known Kit as long as you have, Meg. Normally, she's quiet and shy. Even withdrawn. She doesn't like confrontation or upheaval. Maybe the drinking makes her brave, able to face things. I think it's that way with most people."

"Is that why Linda used to drink?"

"Our marriage had its rough spots. Linda didn't want to deal with the problems, and I wasn't much help at first. Drinking can be an insidious disease. It disguises itself in socializing and recreational activities. Then, suddenly, when the real world closes in, it becomes your whole life."

"What should I do, Carl?"

"Talk to her. Tell her you're concerned. But don't hope for too much. She may not think she's got a problem."

"My mind's whirling like this wind out here. Let's go back to the shop."

The clock in the dining room chimed twice. Meg looked up in disbelief. Two a.m. She'd been reading the legal documents, letters and notes concerning her grandfather's estate for hours. The package, sent by her attorney as promised, had arrived late that afternoon. It was a confusing jumble of information that annoyed and depressed her.

A car door slammed in the driveway, distracting Meg from her work. Footsteps clicked along the sidewalk and the sound of a key in the door. Kit. Her eyes widened when she saw that Meg was still awake.

"No boat? This your new office?" she asked, slurring her words.

"This is work of a different kind."

"Sorry. I'm a little late."

"And a lot drunk."

"I had a few. Went out after the restaurant closed." She swayed momentarily then regained her balance, staggering to a chair and falling into it just in time. "Whatcha' doin'?"

"Finally got the papers from my lawyer. According to what's here, it's true. My father had a son I never knew about."

Kit's head dropped to her chest. Looking up again she blinked, swiping at the air in front of her face. "Sheesh! What're we gonna do?"

"A few things still bother me. I'm thinking of hiring a private detective."

"Gosh." Kit wavered, then leaned both elbows on the table. "Think I'll have one more drink, then go to bed."

Meg spoke softly with concern. "I don't think you need another drink, Kit. I'm worried about you. You've been drinking a lot lately."

Kit's face registered surprise. "Meg, for God's sake! Can't I have a little fun? Don't be such a stick in the mud."

"Really, Kit. I'm serious. I think your drinking's gotten out of control."

"Bullshit. Just because I have a few drinks with friends. Doesn't mean a damned thing."

"You also drink at home. Alone. During the week, on weekends."

Kit got up, her eyebrows raised, her words bristling with anger. "Listen. Meg, why don't you mind your own business? I'm a big girl now. Can take care of myself. Just like you. Going to bed. Goodnight."

Meg watched her weave and shuffle her way toward the kitchen and back staircase. Finally, she followed Kit and grabbed her by the arm.

"I better help you upstairs. You could fall and hurt yourself."

Kit yanked her arm from Meg's grasp. "God damn it, Meg. I'm fine! Let go of me, will ya?"

"Listen, Kit, you shouldn't be driving in this condition. You're going to end up killing someone else or yourself."

"Fuck you!"

"C'mon, Kit. We should be able to talk about this."

"We never talk. That's the whole fucking problem."

Meg crossed her arms. Kit stared coldly. Finally, Meg stomped away, leaving Kit at the bottom of the stairs. Back in the dining room, she looked at the mound of papers stacked neatly at the edge of her grandmother's antique walnut table. Meg felt a building anger she could no longer control. "Fuck this shit!" With a sweep of her arm the papers flew and fluttered, hitting the floor and sliding away to various parts of the room. She sat down and cried, cursing the family dead for the questions they had left her — and for the answers they had not.

The small village of Siasconset was sedate, the quietude not unusual for a late-May morning. Meg bicycled along the deadened streets that came to life only in summer when a steady influx of tourists, including native islanders looking for an escape from the more populated sections of Nantucket, took over the streets of "'Sconset" to enjoy its quaint charm and peaceful beaches.

Once a community of cod and halibut fishermen,

the village dated back to the 17th century. It was an interconnection of streets lined with tiny cottages. Within six weeks, the painted gray and white clapboard cottages would be blanketed with delicate pink roses. Only about 200 families lived in 'Sconset year-round, sharing a small post office, one market, a restaurant and a few shops all located in a central square.

Beyond the square Meg turned down a narrow lane, passing a row of old one-room fishing shacks recently renovated into residences. At the last cottage on the left Meg stopped, wheeling her bicycle onto a driveway made of crushed white shells.

Meg knocked on the outer door. When no one responded she pounded harder and longer. Finally, the door opened. Standing before her was a whiskered old gentleman, his face weathered, his hands calloused from years of fishing the waters surrounding Nantucket. One of her grandfather's oldest and dearest friends, Nathaniel Murphy was ninety years old. He squinted and smiled as he opened the door, reaching for her hand.

"Why, little Meg Rhyland, 'tis a pleasure to see ye. Please come in."

"Thanks, Nate. Hope I'm not interrupting you."

"Nothin' but the wanderin' thoughts of an old man."

Meg sat down on a musty sofa draped with a green wool blanket. Nate sat across from her, lowering himself carefully into a recliner, its leather covering torn by years of wear. He sighed, a look of weariness and pain on his face. Peering at Meg through silver-rimmed glasses slipping over the bridge of his nose, he smiled and scratched his forehead below the brim of an old fishing cap.

"So, what brings ye ta visit old man Nate, Meg? It's been some months since I've seen ye."

"Sorry I haven't come by lately. I've been wrestling with some family problems. Was hoping you could help me, Nate."

"Lassie, if there's any way old Nate can help ye, he will."

"It's about Papa, Nate. The two of you were good friends. And I was wondering if he ever mentioned the existence of another family member. A person who'd be his grandson."

Nate stared blankly, scratching his forehead again and shaking his head. "Honey, there was only his precious Meg. Ye were Richard's only grandchild — and the apple of his eye. A grandson? Where'd ye ever get that notion?"

"From Papa's lawyer. The story goes that my father had a son by a woman who worked for him in his surgical office. Then, years later, Papa changed his will to include this person in the inheritance I was to receive."

Nate reached for the yellow corn-cob pipe and pouch of tobacco sitting on the nearby table. "Meg, I can tell ye what I know about yer daddy in a few short sentences. It's not much, only what Richard told me. And he didn't talk too much about yer daddy. But I don't want ye ta be upset."

"I won't if it'll help."

"Yer daddy was a good man. A Korean War veteran, an excellent surgeon by all accounts. But if he had a weakness it was in his marriage. Richard tried to reason with him, but it was no good. Yer father had a thing for the ladies. Not always yer mother, I'm afraid. But Richard never mentioned this baby. Never."

"I don't understand why Papa didn't trust me with the decisions he made. Maybe I could've gotten to know my brother."

"Doesn't sound much like Richard to leave his precious granddaughter in the dark about somethin' as important as this. I'm sorry I can't help ye."

"It's been a comfort just talking to you."

"Come back soon, lassie. And let old Nate know what happens."

Meg got up and kissed the old man on the forehead. "Hold down the fort, Nate."

"These days the fort will have ta hold me down. Ye don't get old, Meg. Ye just get tired."

"If that's true, I've been feeling pretty old myself lately."

CHAPTER THREE

Looking down the table at the quiet and sometimes sullen faces Meg grimaced. For twenty minutes she and Kit had sat solemnly in the dining room of the big house as lawyers arranged the confusing paperwork necessary to begin the meeting. The constant shuffling of papers was starting to agitate her. Meg managed a quick smile for Kit, who squeezed Meg's hand underneath the table. It was a welcome sign of moral support.

Meg glanced up, unwillingly drawn to the disturbing presence of Michael Gregory, the man who claimed to be her half-brother. Sitting at the opposite end of the table, he was short and dark-haired, with a permanent scowl. His eyebrows were thick, his jaw bearded. There was an air of self-assurance, independence, confidence about him. His movements were jerky and quick, his gaze endlessly shifting from one side of the table to the other until finally it rested on Meg. Empty, unfriendly, she thought. She quickly glanced toward the ceiling, afraid to acknowledge the stranger who'd suddenly come into her life. His stare was unnerving. It touched the child within — the part of her that didn't know, had never known, the fabric of her life.

A voice finally broke the oppressive silence. "Can we get movin' here, or what?" Michael raised both arms in the air as if to question the wasted passage of time.

"Yes, I think so," Gordon Meyers replied. He directed his comments to Meg and Kit. "Mister Freeland, who represents Mister Gregory, has been bringing me up-to-date on the items we'll be discussing."

"Hey, forget all that stuff. I can save everybody a lot of fuckin' time." Standing to his full height of about five and a half feet, Michael puffed his broad chest out with a disturbing air of importance. "I want half of everything my granddaddy left me. What's rightfully mine — what was rightfully my mother's. Nothing more. Nothing less." He glared at Meg. "This family put my mother through absolute hell for years. She died broken-hearted. I'm only sorry she's not alive to witness this victory."

"Michael, please. Let's proceed as we discussed," Freeland insisted. "Miss Rhyland may be perfectly willing to concede to your claim as the law allows. Let's hear what she and her counsel have to say."

Michael extended his right arm, shaking a stubby finger at Meg. "I don't give a shit what Meg Rhyland has to say. It won't change a damned thing. By the way, what's she doing here?" Michael indicated Kit with a wave of his hand.

Gordon Meyers swung abruptly in his chair, running his hand nervously alongside his head. "May I remind you, Mister Gregory, that my client very graciously consented to a meeting in her home so that this matter could be attended to fairly and equitably. I think your manner is insulting, to say the least, and I suggest you sit down."

"This is also my home, buster." Once again, Michael cocked his head toward Kit. "I asked a question. What's she got to do with anything?"

"Miss Stone lives in this house and is a friend of the family's." Meyer's eyes narrowed. "As I suggested before, Mister Gregory, perhaps you should sit down and let us proceed."

"She's got no goddamned business being here, whoever she is. The will doesn't mention her, does it?"

"No, Mister Gregory. But the will mentions my name." Meg stood, fingers nervously tapping the table top. "Due to that fact I'll choose whomever I please to be here. Why make this an unfriendly discussion? Your bad attitude isn't accomplishing anything."

"Well, if I've got a bad attitude you can blame our dear, departed father. He treated my mother like dirt. Me like I didn't exist. I've waited a long time to say what's been on my mind —"

"Excuse me, Miss Rhyland," Freeland said,

interrupting his client. "I think I underestimated the concern Mister Gregory has over these matters. Perhaps a face-to-face discussion isn't possible. It seems that these issues may have to be settled through the mail or in court."

"Don't wimp out on me, Freeland! I want this goddamned deal done now!" Michael took a long look around the room. "In fact, I kinda like this house. Think I'll move in — since it's half mine anyway." He smirked at Meg. "And there's not a fuckin' thing you can do to stop me."

Meg was enraged. "That's it. You're out of here. I don't have to put up with this."

"You'll hear from us soon, Gordon," Freeland said, getting up from his chair. "Miss Rhyland, I apologize for this deplorable waste of time. Now, if you'll excuse us."

"You'll be hearing from me all right," Michael threatened with a sneer. "And don't be surprised when you see me on your goddamned doorstep."

Meg and Kit sat in stunned silence as Michael and Freeland left, escorted to the door by Gordon. When Gordon returned to the table Meg couldn't restrain her outrage.

"What kind of circus are you running here, Gordon? That was inexcusable!"

"Meg, calm down. I've got control over some things, but not Michael Gregory's behavior."

"Can you at least give us a rundown of where we stand with this situation?"

"Listen, Meg, you and Gordon have to talk. You

don't need me in the way." Kit got up, moving toward the living room. "Anyone need a drink?"

"No, thank you," Gordon replied.

Meg frowned in disgust. "No."

"I'll talk to you later, Meg. Nice to have seen you, Gordon."

Gordon rose from his chair. "My pleasure, Kit."

Meg watched her leave, then said, "So, what's the story, Gordon?"

Gordon Meyers rubbed his finger between his shirt collar and necktie. "It's fairly clear, Meg, that the house will have to be redeeded to include both yours and Mister Gregory's name."

Meg squirmed in her chair. "That's it? I lose half the house just like that? Can't we go to court? Fight this thing?"

"On what legal basis, Meg? Certainly we can go to court. But in my professional opinion, it's a waste of time and money. Better to take the loss as it is rather than make it a bigger loss and gain nothing."

"Is Gregory willing to sell his half of the property?"

"According to his lawyer, yes. The property, land and house has been assessed at one million, four hundred thousand dollars."

"And the trust fund?"

Gordon cleared his throat. "I'm afraid that money's tied up and won't be available for at least eight to ten weeks."

Meg shoved her chair back from the table. "Damnit! What's the hold-up on that?"

"Paperwork. Red tape. The usual. In the meantime, Mister Gregory needs a place to live and has decided to reside on this property."

"Here? He really wants to stay here?"

"I'm afraid so."

"Gordon, there must be some way to stop him."

"Not that I'm aware of, Meg."

"Listen, Gordon — you're supposed to be my lawyer. Do something!"

"I'm trying, Meg. But I can't break the law. Half this property belongs to Michael Gregory now. I'll talk to Freeland and see what I can do."

"You said you were going to give me an up-to-date accounting of the trust fund. Do you have those figures?"

"Yes." Gordon shuffled through a stack of papers. "The fund currently amounts to just shy of two million dollars. Your share, of course, would be half. More than enough to purchase Mister Gregory's interest in the property."

"One last thing. All of this paperwork you sent me. The investigations, copies of the will, property deeds and other information. Who on your staff arranged that mess?"

"Mess?"

"Right. It took me hours to get it organized. What am I paying you people for anyway?"

"I'm sorry, Meg. I was unaware of the situation. But I can promise you I'll look into it. Do you need help with anything now?"

"Just get Michael Gregory off my back. And keep him away from this house!"

Late that afternoon, Meg went through the motions of preparing dinner, unable to stop herself from thinking about the meeting. At seven the doorbell rang and Kit went to answer it.

"You're as beautiful as ever!" Brad Hanson kissed Kit on the forehead. "The loveliest eyes on the continent."

Kit laughed and closed the door. "You must be spending too much time in old musty mansions. Something to drink?"

"Whatever you're having will be fine."

Kit back-stepped toward the kitchen. "Two scotches. Coming right up."

Meg sipped a Diet Pepsi, sitting cross-legged on the sofa. Still devastated by the meeting that morning.

Brad kissed Meg's cheek. "Hey, sweetie. You look a little down, to say the least."

Meg sighed, looking toward the ceiling. "Had a meeting with Meyers today. And my charming half-brother."

"What happened?" Brad sank into the sofa and began to caress Meg's back just below the neckline.

"Ahhh. That feels good."

"Tell me about the meeting."

Meg wrung her hands. "This Gregory guy's threatening to move in."

Brad jerked back. "Into the house with you and Kit?"

"Yes. Kit and I'll have to move to the boat."

"Christ. That's absurd." Brad put his arm around her shoulder. "Is there anything I can do? Like bash this guy's face in? I can't believe this is happening."

"The whole story just doesn't fit, Brad. My grandfather would've consulted me about something so serious as another heir to the estate."

"Maybe he didn't want to alarm you. Or hurt you. After all, the situation does shed some negative light on your father's character. Kind of hard to break that to a granddaughter."

"I can't pretend to know what my grandfather was thinking. It's just such a shock."

"Well, maybe Meyers can reason with Gregory. At least convince him not to move in."

"Trust me, Brad. Michael Gregory's not someone you reason with. He's a creep of the first order. And to think he might be my brother . . ."

Kit bounced into the living room, handing Brad his drink. "The lasagna's about ready, Meg. Your timer's down to five minutes."

Meg got up and kissed Brad's cheek. "The cook is needed in the kitchen. No more nasty talk tonight. Let's just enjoy."

After dinner Kit put some music on the stereo. "Hey, let's liven this party up a little!"

Drink in hand, she started to dance — a slinking, fluid-like body motion that raised Meg's eyebrows. Any other time she would've found it sexy. But Kit was drunk and Meg was embarrassed.

"Kit, maybe we should play cards. That is, if Brad's still the card shark he used to be."

Brad bounded across the room toward Kit. "The hell with cards. If Kit wants to dance I'm game. In my line of work my clients are either old, rich and dried-up or young, rich and frigid." Brad took Kit's hand, joining her in the sensuous dance.

"C'mon, Meg. Loosen up, sweetie. Join us."

Meg frowned. The entire day slammed against a wall of despair inside her. "No thanks. I'll watch."

Kit continued her undulating movements, circling Brad, eyes peppering him with seductive glances. Every once in a while, Kit giggled, tripping into Brad's arms.

Meg sat stiffly brooding. Silently, she was amazed at the power of alcohol to change Kit's persona. From shy to outgoing. Quiet to brazen. Careful to reckless. From someone she'd known to someone she didn't.

The next morning, Sandy Russell sat in the kitchen eyeing Meg over the rim of her coffee cup. Meg felt like an amoeba under a microscope with Sandy, the mad scientist, squinting into the lens with sinister intentions. Sandy, Kit's sister, was visiting from Florida. She'd been staying in Boston with other family and had arrived at the big house for an overnight visit. Kit was still upstairs sleeping, recovering from last night's hangover.

Sandy flipped her auburn hair over one shoulder. "Well, I'm not surprised Kit's been drinking."

"You're not?" Meg buttered a cold piece of toast.

"No. She's clearly unhappy. Being in this situation, I mean."

"This situation?" Meg re-buttered the same toast, wondering whether it was hard enough to throw.

"My sister's not a . . ." Sandy leaned forward, whispering, as though her words might float clear

57

across the ocean to a larger populace. "She's not a lesbian, for God's sake. That's why she's drinking. Kit calls me, you know."

"I'm aware of that."

"And she's utterly miserable. What the hell are you doing to her anyway?"

"What am I doing to her?" Meg didn't like the insinuation.

"Yes. What?"

"I love her, Sandy. We're lovers."

Sandy's face turned apple-red. "God, please. Spare me the details."

"Look, if you want details — meaningful ones, I can tell you that Kit's been under a lot of pressure at the restaurant. And I've got some serious legal troubles."

"Legal troubles?" Sandy shot up from her chair. "I didn't know they could send you to jail for this! What about Kit? She's perfectly innocent!"

Meg stopped chewing her toast. "Sandy, what're you talking about?"

Sandy grabbed the back of the chair for support. "Lesbians. Can they send you to jail?"

Meg laughed. She couldn't help it — even when Sandy flashed her a look of pure disdain. "Sandy, I was talking about this house. My grandfather's will. He passed away in February."

"You didn't answer my question."

"Didn't I?"

Sandy put her coffee cup in the kitchen sink. She leaned against the counter, her stone-washed jeans and burgundy T-shirt outlining an attractive figure. "Can they send you to jail for corrupting my sister? For sleeping with women?"

"In some states. They're probably watching the house as we speak." Meg raised her eyebrows and smiled. "Guess you're on the list now too."

Sandy's eyeballs bulged.

"Only kidding."

"That's very sadistic, Meg." A finger wagged in Meg's direction. "Don't make fun of my concern for Kit."

"Then stop the crap, Sandy. This isn't about who Kit sleeps with. It's about a disease, an illness."

"Kit needs to get away from here. From you, quite frankly."

"She needs professional counseling. It might help if you'd talk to her."

"Already have."

"About the drinking?"

"Yes. I'm very worried about it too. I'll talk to her again."

Meg pushed her plate away. "Thank you."

Sandy crossed her arms and said, "Kit loves you. I know that. But she's also confused. About who she is and what she wants. She's always been isolated. Hard to communicate with."

"I know."

"She didn't get along with my parents. She was thirteen when they got divorced. I'd already gone away to college. I'm afraid she got the worst of it."

"She's told me bits and pieces."

"Getting away would do her good. I've invited her to Florida to stay with me for a while."

"What did she say?"

"That she'd think about it."

* * * * *

The Nantucket ferry lurched heavily forward. Meg stood undercover on the lower deck, peering at the ocean through a rain-drizzled window. The afternoon light quickly faded from gray to black, dark storm clouds blocking what light remained. A sudden swell lifted the ferry, tossing her roughly backward. She grabbed the metal railing and held on tightly, regaining her balance as the ferry settled back into the water. Meg tried to blink away the stab of panic she felt rising from within. It was always the same panic. She feared the ocean, and she still wondered why her grandfather had never taken her out before she was thirteen.

"No, Papa! I don't want to go!"

She felt the arms of her grandfather around her, then he took her gently by the hand. "Meg, the boat's not dangerous. You'll have fun once you're aboard."

"But what if the boat crashes? Or sinks?" They'd read about the *Titanic* in school, and there were stories of fishermen lost at sea.

"Well, young lady, it's a beautiful day and I happen to be an excellent sailor."

Meg reluctantly followed him, walking quickly to keep up with his long strides, her hand still held tightly within his own. When they reached the end of the dock, he helped her up the ramp onto the boat's deck. Her knees felt like jelly. Her grandfather was quickly alongside her, his hands on her shoulders as they edged toward the boat's outer railings.

"Meg, the *Emily*'s one of the finest boats in Nantucket. And I'm going to keep refitting her until one day she belongs to you."

Meg heard the pride in her grandfather's voice, a voice that was also comforting, strong. She looked around the boat and saw what her grandfather saw; the *Emily* was beautiful, gleaming in the sun's bright light. She could barely feel the swell of the water beneath her. But what about the giant rocks around the island? And the huge waves when storms came? She looked up at her grandfather. His face seemed hopeful. She didn't want to make him sad. It was rare that he had time to take her anywhere. How could she say no?

"You know I don't like the ocean, Papa. It's . . . I don't know — spooky. Dark and scary."

"Dark? Scary? Look out there. The ocean's blue. As blue as your eyes."

Meg looked at the endless water. It was blue. Not like she'd sometimes seen it. Once it'd been almost black. As angry as the wind, splashing in huge waves along the beach. Crashing like thunder. "What if a storm comes?"

"The weather's perfect. We can go for a ride up the coast to the lighthouse."

"I don't like the lighthouse much anymore. But I'll go with you for the ride."

He took both her hands, then squeezed and kissed them. "I know you don't like the lighthouse, Meg. Or the ocean. Sometimes things happen to make us afraid. But nothing will hurt you today. Promise."

"Guess everyone but me likes the ocean."

"Maybe you've got good reason not to like it. But time passes. We do the best we can."

That day she stayed on the boat with her grandfather. The *Emily* cut through the water with ease; Meg's hair blew against her face, tangling in the wind. Everything she saw was beautiful... the rocks along the shoreline, the big white sea birds, the tiny lighthouse that grew bigger and bigger, the billowing clouds like floating white islands in the sky. Her grandfather let her take the steering wheel and when she grabbed it, she felt a power she'd never known. The power to go anywhere — to steer herself in any direction.

From that day on Meg loved the *Emily* — because it kept her safe from the water. Because it took her where she wanted to go. But she was afraid of the ocean the boat lived on — an unconscious fear she could never quite explain. When the ocean was angry she stayed away. When the ocean was peaceful she stayed on the boat ... wary, but undefeated.

Her grandfather was proud of her love for the *Emily,* proud that she'd found the courage to face her fears. Nothing else about the *Emily* frightened her. She'd learned to navigate, learned to sail through the narrowest channels and around the rockiest underwater cliffs. She accompanied her grandfather on fishing trips, enjoyed picnics on deck. When she was older she sometimes hosted parties and cooked special dinners in the *Emily*'s galley. But when it came time for the guests or her grandfather to swim, Meg clung to the boat for safety. She saw the water below as a monstrous phantom that would surely suck her under. As long as she stayed on board she'd be safe.

One day, after her twenty-first birthday — complete with a party held aboard the *Emily* — she hugged her grandfather and thanked him. The *Emily,* she'd told him, was her favorite place in the whole world.

"One thing I promise you," he'd said, "the *Emily* will someday be yours. No matter what else happens you'll always have the *Emily.*"

The Nantucket ferry bounced wildly once again, her grandfather's words still echoing, "No matter what else happens . . . No matter what else happens . . ."

Her grandfather had kept his promise. Gordon Meyers had told her, hadn't he? In every legal document the *Emily* was willed specifically to her and her alone. But what had her grandfather's words really meant spoken over twenty years ago? "No matter what else happens . . ."

Loud music from the room adjoining the bar muffled nearby conversations. A video game from behind shrieked and beeped as a patron operated its controls. Two women kissed in a shadowy corner. The bartender washed glasses and opened bottles of beer with the heel of his hand. One of those beers was for Meg, who'd chosen a bar stool with a good view of the door.

As she sat, an army of thoughts sounded a cadence through her head. Kit's drinking was growing steadily worse, straining their relationship when other strains were already inflicting damage. Michael

Gregory was still threatening to move into the big house. The new shop opened in five weeks requiring complete attention and, as always, more money. Meyers moved slowly, mired in paperwork and, in her mind, inefficiency.

Suddenly the door to the outside world opened, letting in a rush of late-May air. Meg blinked several times, the cool air bringing a heady jolt to incinerating thoughts. A woman approached, striding along the bar at a brisk pace. She was of medium build, all her bodily curves hidden by a calf-length black raincoat, it's collar turned up.

She stopped about two feet from Meg's stool. Droplets of water ran from the coat's epaulets and pooled onto the floor. She squinted slightly. "Evening. Meg Rhyland?"

"Yes." Meg's hand was firmly gripped and vigorously shaken.

"Susan Marks. Nice to meet you."

"Care for a drink?"

"Yeah, fine." Susan Marks removed her coat and sat down, the curves now showing. She was an attractive woman, naturally beautiful with gray-black eyes the color of storm clouds. Dark hair, styled short in soft curls, dripped rainwater onto the bar. She removed a small spiral notebook from her front shirt pocket and opened it to the first empty page. Resting her elbow on the bar, Susan scribbled several illegible lines with a Bic pen held at an odd angle between the thumb and first two fingers of her left hand. "So, you want someone investigated?"

Meg nervously tapped her fingers on the counter's smooth surface. "That's correct."

"I'll need details."

Susan Marks was all business. Meg liked her immediately. Reaching down, Meg removed a manila envelope from her briefcase on the floor. "I've got a file folder with all the information you'll need, including a detailed report on a prior investigation conducted on the same individual and other involved parties about fifteen years ago."

Susan removed the contents. "Mmmm. Interesting."

As Susan continued writing and reading, Meg continued staring. She had a strong build — clearly she worked out at a gym. But there was something delicate about her too. A softness that seemed out of place. Suddenly, Meg thought she'd seen Susan before. There was a familiarity about her, a structure to Susan's face that Meg recognized.

"Have we met before?" Meg asked, still unsure.

Susan looked up and smiled. The skin around her eyes crinkled pleasantly. She had a thin face and strong jaw. Her tone was decisive. "I've seen you before. At a few of the clubs in Provincetown. You live on the island, don't you?"

"Since I was six."

"I was born there. Then my family moved to Boston. Lived there for almost twenty years. I moved back to the island about five years ago."

Meg managed a half-smile of her own. "I can't quite believe I'm doing this — hiring a private investigator." At least she felt in charge now. Despite doubts and misgivings she'd decided to take Hollis's advice. If she made a fool of herself no one needed to know besides Kit and Hollis — and they'd seen the fool in her many times.

"Miss Rhyland . . ."

"Meg's fine. No need to be formal."

"That goes both ways. Meg, there's some pretty detailed information in this file. I'm going to need time to look it over."

"When will I hear from you?"

"I'll check in on a weekly basis." A look of concern crossed Susan's face. "But it's never a good idea to talk over the phone. We should set up a standard meeting place each week. An isolated spot."

"We can meet on my boat. I'll write down the docking address for you."

"Fine. Say we meet every Saturday evening at eight o'clock until I have some answers for you." Meg agreed and Susan continued, "Don't blame you for taking this action, Meg. There's a lot at stake here. I'll see what I can find out about Mister Gregory. And in the meantime, try not to worry. By my observations it doesn't appear you've been getting much sleep."

"I haven't," Meg said ruefully. She drained the last of her beer and put out her hand. "Maybe the investigation will help. Thanks, Susan."

The Back Alley Tavern was crowded for a Thursday night. Meg stood patiently in the lobby, scanning the large room to her right, looking for Kit. She was impressed by the recent renovations. The old-time tavern-style appearance had been meticulously maintained with brass fixtures, wide oak ceiling beams, textured walls and the flicker of candlelight. Harpoons, whale bones, rum kegs, ropes and netting were now displayed throughout the rooms in honor of the fishing and whaling industries which dominated Cape Cod, Nantucket and the surrounding area in the mid-1800's. Kit had done a wonderful job helping to develop the construction plans and supervise the renovations. The changes were effective, the atmosphere inviting.

Acoustical guitar music drifted in from the main dining room; laughter could be heard from the nearby bar and wine cellar; a waiter rushed past with a full tray of frosted beer mugs.

Finally Rick, the maitre d', greeted her, escorting her by the arm toward the bar. "How lovely you look tonight! Waiting for Kit? Think she's still in the bar talking to some of the regulars. A little PR never hurts."

"Comes with the territory."

Once in the bar, she spotted Kit immediately, sitting on a barstool in the middle of a long line of men and women who were both standing and sitting. For some minutes Meg remained in the background, watching the group a few yards away. They were all drinking — laughing as Kit entertained them with stories about the restaurant's renovations and a special open house planned for the following weekend. Meg could hardly believe her eyes. This was not the Kit she knew — quiet, soft-spoken, reticent. It was that other person — outgoing, brash, lighthearted, almost reckless. It was a transformation that stunned her again and again.

With some hesitation, Meg stepped toward the

group of strangers. "Kit," she said, tapping Kit's arm. "Excuse me for interrupting. But we're still having dinner tonight, aren't we?"

Kit swiveled toward Meg, her face blank. "Meg, what're you doing here?"

"Thought we were having dinner tonight."

"Dinner? Tonight? I don't remember . . ."

"Well, when you're done with your story I'll be in the lobby waiting." Meg left the bar angry, hurt. Standing in the lobby, she reluctantly reached for the front door.

"Meg, wait. I'm sorry." Kit grabbed Meg's hand. "I forgot, it's true. But I've been preoccupied with the reopening and the open house next weekend. Please, don't leave."

Meg did a one-eighty and focused on Kit. "I agree you've been preoccupied." She lowered her voice. "Mostly with drinking and, yes, also with the restaurant. It's obvious there's no time left for me."

"Meg, that's not true. We've both been busy."

"Well, I remembered tonight, didn't I? We were both supposed to celebrate the opening of the new shop and restaurant with a quiet romantic dinner. But you chose to start celebrating without me — in a manner you've grown accustomed to lately. Goodnight."

Meg opened the door and left without looking back. Looking back was something she'd come to despise in any form.

CHAPTER FOUR

Following a long corridor from the annex, Meg reached the old section of the Boston Public Library. Opened in 1895, the original library was built around a quiet courtyard complete with flower gardens and a fountain. Beyond the courtyard Meg found the old building's main entrance hall. Passing two enormous stone lions commemorating Massachusetts' regiments during the Civil War, Meg took the stairs leading to Bates Hall. The hall, hundreds of feet long, was the library's main reference reading room. The musty smell of old books, a quiet shuffling of papers, the sound of footsteps down long aisles and the rhythmic clicking of computer keys echoed throughout the large room. Its high, barrel-arched ceiling made her dizzy.

Meg stood in line at the reference desk, waiting to talk to a librarian. She eyed her watch impatiently. Only two hours to spare before the pottery exhibit opened downtown.

"Can I help you, miss?"

"I'd like to see some old newspapers — past issues of the *Globe*."

"Year?"

"Nineteen sixty-one."

"Everything's stored on microfiche. Let's see what we can find for you."

Meg followed the librarian to a nearby corner where several microfiche-viewing machines were located. The librarian, a short plump woman, unlocked a shelf cabinet and peered inside. "Know how to use the machines?"

"Yes."

"This should do it for you. Follow the instructions on the outside of the case. If you have any other questions, just ask."

Meg sat down and inserted the cartridge into the machine. Flipping the switch, the machine whirred softly, its green screen turning white.

There were several years of the *Globe* on one cartridge — 1960 to 1962. Meg quickly scanned through 1960 into 1961. The months of January, February and March passed before her — words from the era blurring by like a speeding time machine. When she reached April, she slowed down, paging carefully until she came to April 23, 1961 — the day her life changed forever. With all the fortitude she could muster, she reached into the past, a low agonizing moan passing between her lips. Black bold headlines on the lower half of the morning edition's front page caused a trickle of sweat to run from the top of her forehead to the bridge of her nose: *"Boston Surgeon and Wife Killed in Early Morning Accident."*

Meg closed her eyes, then opened them again. The words were still there, etched in time. What had always been her own surrealistic nightmare was suddenly very real. Black words on a page. An objective accounting of history. She'd never been told the facts, had never known how or why the accident happened. It had simply been called "the accident." Her parents had gone to heaven; she'd be living with her grandfather. No details for a child not yet six, and she'd never asked.

Meg fought against a wave of emotion pressing from within. Fear. Hurt. Abandonment. Insides churning, she willed herself to read the front-page story written 35 years ago.

"An early morning accident claimed the lives of a Massachusetts General Hospital surgeon and his wife on Charles Street in the West End section of the city. Dr. James R. Rhyland and his wife, Anne M. Seager Rhyland, were pronounced dead at the scene by Boston city coroner, William J. Eckhardt.

Dr. Rhyland was driving the vehicle, which officials say skidded and struck a utility pole on the corner of Fruit and Charles streets near Massachusetts General Hospital.

Mrs. Rhyland, riding in the front passenger seat, was killed instantly after being thrown almost thirty feet from the vehicle. Dr. Rhyland was freed from the automobile after ambulance drivers worked for more than forty-five minutes, hampered by the rainstorm. Crews from Boston Edison were called to de-energize a live electric line dislodged from the pole during the accident. Dr. Rhyland was pronounced dead at the scene a short time later.

Officials gave this version of the accident:

The Rhyland vehicle was proceeding south on Charles Street at approximately three a.m. at a high rate of speed. The car lost control, skidded on the wet street and slid sideways into a utility pole located at the intersection of Charles and Fruit streets. The vehicle wrapped itself around the pole, downing a high-voltage power line. The vehicle's passenger side windows exploded on impact and Mrs. Rhyland was thrown from the passenger seat onto the roadway.

Damage to the utility pole caused a power outage at Massachusetts General, forcing the hospital to activate its back-up generator.

An eyewitness to the accident, unidentified by police, claimed to have seen a second vehicle chasing the Rhyland car, causing it to lose control. The alleged vehicle failed to stop and continued south on Charles to Cambridge Street.

The Rhylands are survived by a daughter, Megan

S. Rhyland, 5. Services are being arranged by the Foster Funeral Home, Beacon Hill."

Meg blinked furiously, trying to hold back tears. She jotted a few notes and turned off the machine. Mother thrown from the vehicle. Died instantly. Father trapped for forty-five minutes. Still alive. Dies a short time later. And, if that wasn't shocking enough, there had been a witness. A witness who saw another car chasing them, causing the crash. It was a piece of information that shocked her, bringing with it the notion that her parent's accident may never have been an accident at all.

There was a crack of lightning followed by an explosion of thunder. Lights inside the boat flickered, then gave way to darkness. Meg looked out the cabin window across the bow. It was completely black, the shoreline indistinguishable, all other boat slips dark.

After five minutes of continuous darkness Meg grabbed a kerosene lamp from the cabinet above the galley sink. Once lit the lamp cast an eerie glow up the starboard wall to the ceiling. The on-shore generator that provided power to the boat slips had been knocked out by lightning, Meg guessed. The *Emily* had its own power source, a small generator controlled from the upper deck console. But Meg didn't move to activate it. The kerosene lamp would do fine.

Staring out the window again, Meg watched the June storm and tried not to think about the events of the last several weeks. Rain pelted the rooftop and deck — a loud drumbeat in between crashes of thunder. Then a shadow moved. Seemingly undaunted by wind and rain, the shadow appeared to glide along the starboard side of the boat. Several times as it edged its way toward the upper cabin door, the dark image shimmered, reflecting the sharp flashes of lightning streaking across the horizon.

Meg heard the upper cabin door open. The sound of the storm rushed in, bringing the shadow with it. The dark form stood at the bottom of the steps — dripping hat and poncho spraying a shower of rainwater across the wooden floor.

"Hope I didn't startle you — but the wind brought me in, literally." The granite-gray eyes of Susan Marks took on the glow of the room, an orange glow like the eyes of a cat in a dimly lit alleyway. She blinked and smiled, no longer a shadow but rather a strong presence caught by the glow of lamplight. "Nice to see you again, Meg."

With effort Meg pulled herself from the trance-like state the woman seemed to infuse. "Let me take your hat and poncho. I'll hang them up in the bathroom. What about your shoes?"

Susan looked down at her feet. Taking a few steps backward, the shoes sloshed with rain water. "Mmmm, yes. Better come off too."

When Meg returned she found Susan sitting at the salon's dining room table lighting a cigarette. It was their third meeting on the boat, and Meg was anxious to hear any updates on the investigation.

Susan flicked a small silver lighter twice, the blue flame singeing her cigarette on the second try. "Sorry I'm late." She looked at her watch. "Two hours late." "Quite a storm out there." Meg smiled. "Can I offer you a drink?"

"Coffee if you have some. Need something warm."

"Sure." Meg went to the galley and filled the percolator.

"Didn't think you'd make it at all."

"I was beginning to wonder myself."

"Usually the shore road closes in weather like this. That's why I thought you might not get here . . ." She set the creamer, sugar and mugs on a tray and brought it into the salon.

"I'm here," Susan replied. She looked at the table next to the sofa. On it, Meg displayed framed photographs of friends and family. "I meant to ask you before — who's the soldier?" She picked up a picture of Brad.

"Brad Hanson. An old friend. He's like a brother to me. That picture was taken while he was in the Army reserves some years ago."

"Strong face. Good-looking." Susan touched a second frame. "And this must be Kit."

"Yes. We've been together over four years."

"Lovely." As Meg poured coffee into the mugs, Susan plopped some soggy-looking files onto the table. "Want to bring you up-to-date on the investigation." She crossed her legs as a long exhale of smoke clouded her face. "Finally finished reviewing the legal documents you gave me. Seems like this guy Gregory has a legitimate claim all right — at least on paper. But I'm not finished with this investigation yet.

75

Here's why." Susan opened a file. She pointed to the empty space on the sofa. "Sit here. Need to show you something."

Meg sat down. A perfume-like scent drifted from Susan — a freshness that pleasantly obliterated the smell of smoke. "Find something?"

Susan smiled, eyebrows raised. "Maybe. As you know, I've been shadowing Mister Gregory on-and-off for the past few weeks. I told you last time we met that he lives on Martha's Vineyard?"

"Yes."

"Well, here're some photos. Nice house, huh? Too nice for a two-bit insurance salesman. So I dug a little further. As I suspected, Mister Gregory doesn't own this house. Not sure he even sells insurance. He's supposed to have his own business but doesn't seem to work much. Anyway, the house is owned by some guy named Luis Raphael."

"Who's he?"

Susan leaned back, resting an arm behind her head. "Don't really know. In fact, no one seems to know. I'm having him checked out too. Right now what's interesting to me is Gregory himself. I ran a credit check on him — very routine. Look at this report." Susan's index finger trailed down the page. "Not long ago he reserved three one-way tickets to Brazil. Charged them to his Visa account. Checked with the airline. He's scheduled to leave within a couple of months."

"One-way, huh? Interesting."

"I thought so. Wonder why he wants to leave the country? I mean, he did threaten to move into your house."

Meg sipped her coffee. "He did."

"Guess he doesn't plan to hang around too long. Another thing about the credit check. Usually, you can go back seven years on someone. His history goes back less than two years. All of his accounts were opened in the last eighteen months. I think that's strange."

"Sounds odd. Especially for a guy his age."

"In my opinion, there's good cause to continue this investigation." Susan ran her hand through her jet-black hair. One stray curl dropped over her forehead. "Your instincts are good, Meg. Gregory may not be what he seems."

"More coffee?"

"Yes, thanks."

Meg returned with the pot. "I've been doing a little research myself. Like to tell you about it."

"I'm all ears."

Meg took the next ten minutes to explain her recent trip to the Boston Public Library and what she'd found out about her parent's accident, the mystery witness and the second unidentified vehicle.

"Well, that news must've startled you." Susan looked directly at her. For the first time Meg consciously acknowledged the pristine face, powerful eyes. "I've got some contacts at the Boston PD. Might be able to get my hands on the original police report. Could help fill in a few blanks."

"I hope so. My life seems full of blanks."

A bright flash followed by a loud thunder clap interrupted the conversation. Meg heard waves washing over the deck above, felt the boat rock unsteadily in the water. The wind moaned, then the kerosene lamp flickered into darkness. Meg felt her way toward the lamp. It was out of fuel, completely empty.

"I'll have to put the back-up generator on." Meg turned toward Susan. "You may want to stay aboard tonight. Roads will definitely be closed now," she said, talking at the darkness.

A steady voice from the blackness answered. "I've had enough of storms tonight. Thanks for the invitation."

"You can sleep in the forward bedroom. It's small, but comfortable."

"Show me the way."

Meg felt a hand on her shoulder. The touch was firm and somehow comforting.

"Must we wait for lights?" Susan asked.

"No. Follow me."

Meg shuffled slowly toward the forward cabin. "There's a flashlight in the dresser. You'll need it until the generator kicks in." Opening the top drawer, Meg fumbled for the flashlight. She switched it on and swung around. No one was there. "Susan?" Stepping backwards, Meg tripped over her own feet landing squarely on the bed in Susan's lap.

The surprised woman laughed, grabbing Meg tenderly at the waist. "Well, hello."

With a gentle push, Susan helped Meg up. Turning around, Meg surrendered the light. "Sorry, I'm not usually so clumsy."

Susan leaned back on her elbows, smiling broadly. "How could I possibly object? It's not every day a beautiful woman falls into my lap."

Meg felt herself blush. "If you need anything, let me know."

As the lightning flashed, so did Susan's eyes. "I will."

Meg slept well that night, and the following morning sunlight burst through every cabin window. Fully dressed and feeling invigorated after a shower, she made coffee in the galley. A few minutes later she rapped lightly on Susan's bedroom door. When there was no response she knocked louder. "Susan? You up? Like some coffee?" No response. Meg opened the door. As the crack widened she peeked into the room. "Susan?" The room was empty, the bed made as if no one had ever spent the night. The stern investigator was gone — not a trace remaining of her presence.

From the living room of the big house loud music drifted outside. For an hour Meg had been sitting on the deck, staring at the seascape — the gradual sloping of land toward ocean. A rocky shoreline that finally, almost unwillingly, gave way to the pounding of the water. Above the rocks, the sea grasses blew, shimmering golden in the sunlight. And above the grasses, the yard, molded into patches of lawn and garden by human hands. A gentleness that didn't quite belong.

Nothing seemed to belong. For the past two months Meg's life had slowly unraveled, baring raw nerves she'd never acknowledged. Her conscious moments had been overtaken by a shadow-filled past, an unknown family member, a private investigator, lawyers and a strained relationship with Kit. Her life seemed to be running like sand through her fingers

— scattered particles she could no longer hold onto. What more could possibly happen?

"Going to sit here all night?" Kit took the seat across from her.

"Maybe." Meg immediately noticed the drink in Kit's hand. It was a common fixture.

"Where were you all day yesterday?"

"At the boat. Then the storm hit and I stayed the night."

"Was that a smart thing to do?" Kit snapped.

Meg looked at the glistening bloodshot eyes — no longer as blue as she once remembered. "Better than trying to drive home in it."

"Did that investigator ever show up?"

"Yes. Barely made it in the storm."

"Any news?"

"Some."

Kit slouched forward in the chair. "What kind of answer is that?"

"The investigation's just underway. Susan's got a lot more digging to do."

"Susan? Getting a little friendly, aren't we?" Kit sat back, crossing her legs. There was a coldness in her voice Meg hadn't heard before.

"I've only met the woman four or five times, Kit. And believe me, she's strictly business."

"But you're on a first-name basis, nonetheless."

"What would you have me call her? Miss Marks? That sounds ridiculous."

"I don't think so." Finishing her drink, Kit shoved the arm holding the glass toward Meg. "And if she managed to make it home in the storm why didn't you?"

"She didn't make it home, Kit."

Kit's arm shot out to the side in an angry gesture, ice flying out of the glass. The ice skidded across the deck onto the sand. "Well, wasn't that cozy?"

"It wasn't. Please. I'm not in the mood for any nonsense right now. I've got enough problems."

"Finding company isn't one of them."

"Well, maybe I need some company. Especially since you've taken up your new hobby."

Looks of disgust and bitterness distorted Kit's face. "What's that supposed to mean?"

"Your drinking, Kit. I think we've had this discussion before. I'm worried sick about you."

"Why don't you stop the shit and let me help you?"

"Kit, the best thing you can do for me is help yourself."

"Oh, brother. Push me away — just like you always do. Meg Rhyland, the invincible."

"Invincible?" Meg threw her hands up in the air. "Can't you see what the fuck's happening here?"

"You better believe I can."

"Could've fooled me."

Kit laughed sarcastically. "Fuck you, Meg. Living with you hasn't exactly been easy the past few months. Know why?" She got up, swaying over Meg like a wind-blown sapling. "Because Meg Rhyland, the control freak, is losing control. Things are slipping away — and God forbid you should have to depend on anyone. Like me . . . Brad . . . Hollis." Kit placed her hands on her hips. "No. Meg Rhyland doesn't need anyone, including the woman she's lived with for four years."

Meg took her gently by the arm. "Listen, you've

got to get help. The stress of everything is killing us both."

"Nothing's killing me, sweetheart, but boredom."

"Boredom?" Meg looked at her.

"Exactly. I'm thinking of taking a trip to Florida to visit my sister."

Meg tried to be enthusiastic, though the thought of being without Kit, even in her present condition, frightened the hell out of her. But she couldn't say it. She just couldn't. "Kit, I think that's a great idea. Maybe getting away for a while is the answer."

Kit stomped toward the door, opening it part way. "Sure, you'd like to get rid of me, wouldn't you?"

"That's ridiculous. I'd be on that damned plane with you if I could."

"But you can't, of course. Fine. I'll make the arrangements. Now that this restaurant hoopla is over with I can leave next week."

Meg swallowed hard, biting her bottom lip. "Kit, please don't . . ."

"I need to get away."

"I know. But let's at least be hospitable to Brad. He'll be here any minute."

"Thought he was headed back to Europe."

"Just got back. Leaves again next week."

"Maybe I can hitch a ride. There're so many miles between us, a few thousand more wouldn't make any difference."

The door slammed.

During dinner Meg stared at the broiled lemon chicken. Each bite felt like a rock sliding down her throat. Brad was his usual charming self — quietly comforting, trying to talk through the tension. Kit sat stiffly, hardly touching the food, her hand wrapped eternally around the tumbler of scotch.

Brad was rambling on about a trip to Spain. "Madrid's a beautiful city. Auctioned an estate there last summer. The owners were Mediterranean art collectors. Fabulous inventory." He rubbed his fingers together. "These people had money, let me tell you."

In between sips, Kit focused on Brad. "Gosh, I'd love to travel. Meet people. See all those beautiful homes."

Brad smiled. "Well, Kit, maybe someday you can join me. You'd love Paris."

"Who'll show me a good time?" she asked, eyebrows raised.

"Meg can come along. We'll make it a family affair."

Kit laughed, looking across the table at Meg. "A good time for Meg is filling green stamp books."

Brad chuckled. Seeing Meg's flash of annoyance, he cleared his throat and cut into his chicken. "Vienna is next. Then back to London. There's lots to do in both cities — even for the unadventurous."

"Bet you know how to show those European women a good time," Kit commented, sucking on an ice cube.

"Know all the cozy spots — the great views, best restaurants. A few hideaways." Brad tipped his chair until it rested on its back legs. "Of course, dealing with mostly wealthy clients gives me access to some perks here and there. Swanky parties. Fine wines." He nodded toward Kit. "The best scotch. And some pretty high-class suites at the finest resorts."

"I'm terribly impressed," Meg said moodily. "And it appears Kit is too."

"Well, gosh, Meg. What the hell is there to do around here but stare at that overgrown pool out back? It's good to know someone's having an exciting life."

Meg slapped her napkin down on the table. Getting up, she poured herself a brandy — completely resigned to feeling miserable for the rest of the evening. "If you can't beat 'em, join 'em," she said with a wink.

After two drinks of her own Meg excused herself from the living room where Kit and Brad continued to drink and play cards. Upstairs, she fell into a fitful sleep, tossing and turning from one bad dream into the next.

A few hours later, Meg realized her eyes were wide open. Staring across the room, she noticed the time — after two a.m. Turning over, she discovered she was still alone. Kit was still downstairs drinking and playing cards with Brad, no doubt. Tomorrow, she thought, Kit would have a headache much worse than her own.

Meg staggered out of bed to find an aspirin. In the bathroom she turned on the overhead light. Looking straight ahead, she found herself face-to-face with her own reflection. There were dark circles under her eyes, lines across her forehead, around her mouth. She touched her cheek, making sure the reflection was real. This wasn't how she remembered looking. Like everything around her she was changing too.

Pills in one hand, a glass of water in the other, Meg left the mirrored image behind. Rest was what she needed, she told herself. The kind where there was only blackness. No thoughts. No dreams.

In the hallway Meg bumped against the wall, spilling the water. Silently she cursed and took the tablets with the water left in the cup. As she swallowed a low moan filtered down the hallway from somewhere behind her. Startled, she stopped and turned. But the big house made all kinds of sounds —creaking, rattling, echoing lamentations of a structure more than one hundred and fifty years old.

She heard the sound again. A sound that seemed more human than house. She moved slowly toward the door at the opposite end of the hallway. The door was closed. She opened it. Quickly, like a child afraid of the boogie man, she flipped the light switch. In a split second she assimilated the scene before her. Brad thrusting himself into Kit, Kit's arms locked tightly around his back. Then the instant was over and the two stared back at her. Brad in shock. Kit visibly drunk. Not a word spoken.

Meg closed the door. She was dreaming again. Sleepwalking. Vaguely, she remembered Papa's stories about how she had sleepwalked as a child. Bumping into doors, falling down stairs, crying for no reason at all.

She was crying now. It'd been a bad dream. A bad bump in the night. It was only when she woke up to the sun-flooded room that she realized her nights of sleepwalking had long ago passed. What she'd seen last night wasn't a dream.

Meg sat at the bar drinking club soda, trying to

make sense of the previous evening. Kit and Brad. Betrayal. Hurt. The nightmare of it. Two of the people she trusted most. And loved. Still loved. She put both hands to her face. Her eyes burned with the tears.

She'd ventured out to The Breaker hoping to run into Hollis. Unfortunately, she wasn't there. So she sat alone and wallowed — as if there were any other way.

"Hello, Meg."

The voice startled her. She wiped the tears away with the heel of her hand, trying to regain her composure. When she finally looked up it was into the smiling face of Susan Marks. She managed a subdued, "Hello."

Susan's smile changed into an expression of concern. "Meg, you all right?"

"Fine, fine. Just feeling sorry for myself. A bad habit I don't recommend."

"Mind company?"

Meg nodded toward the empty seat next to her.

Susan ordered a beer and turned her chair sideways facing Meg. She raised her arms, palms up. "I don't know why — but something tells me your present state of mind has nothing to do with legal matters. Woman trouble?"

Meg laughed softly. "Either I'm totally transparent — or you're one hell of a mind reader."

"Well, we've all had those problems. When I saw you drooped over the bar like you were the only one in here, I recognized the signs."

Looking at the attractive woman next to her, Meg could hardly imagine Susan with any similar worries. "You're having woman problems too?"

Susan shook her head. "No, not at the moment. I'm presently unattached." Susan swiveled her chair toward the crowded room. "A few years ago I lost someone very special."

"I'm sorry."

"Her name . . ." There was a pause, a flutter in Susan's throat. "Her name was Jan." Susan glanced back at Meg. "We were together for about four years. Then she died of breast cancer."

Meg bowed her head. "Oh, God." It was true. She'd been trying to convince herself earlier that things could be worse. Much worse. "That's awful."

Susan scanned the room. "Anyway, I haven't really gotten back into the dating scene or anything like that. I guess when I meet the right person . . ." She shrugged.

"You must've loved her very much."

"I did." Susan hopped off the bar chair. "Want to dance?"

"Yes." The word leapt from Meg's mouth. She could feel her cheeks redden as Susan reached for her hand.

Susan smiled, obviously amused. "I like decisive women."

Fully convinced she was still dreaming, Meg put her arms around Susan Marks. Last night's "dream" had run into today. Soon she was going to wake up to the creaking sounds of the big house and the aroma of coffee brewing in the kitchen. Kit at the stove standing over sputtering eggs. The morning paper in her hands with its inky smell and limp pages curling over the very headline she wanted to skim. The same boring news, the sameness of everything.

But there was only the light fragrance of Susan's perfume. Flashing strobe lights and loud music covered droning voices. There was a breath across her cheek and the faint smell of alcohol. The warmth of a woman she hardly knew curved perfectly against her — as if they'd danced a hundred dances and would dance a hundred more.

"Feeling any better?" Susan asked, pulling Meg closer.

"Disoriented. I feel disoriented."

"Understood. I've been disoriented for the past three years."

"Then maybe it's good we're dancing — to hold each other up."

"Mmmm, yes. Seems we've both had our slips and falls."

Meg smiled, feeling suddenly safe and not knowing completely why.

CHAPTER FIVE

The following week, Meg sat in the stuffy car, fingers impatiently tapping the steering wheel. Traffic was backed up as far as she could see, jammed solid along the tunnel beneath Boston Harbor. She'd just left Kit at Logan International Airport about fifteen minutes ago, an unpleasant parting that still lingered in the dark stale tunnel.

For some insane reason, Meg had felt the need to be cheerful. She slid Kit's carry-on bag onto the conveyor belt moving slowly toward the X-ray machine. "Any special plans while you're in Florida?"

"Spend time at the beach. Take day trips with my sister."

"Hope it's a relaxing vacation for you, Kit."

"Thanks." Kit turned away, staring out the large window toward the runway. "I'm not the person I thought I was, Meg."

"I don't think either one of us is."

"I've hurt you terribly. And I've hurt and humiliated myself. I need to get away to find some answers."

"We both need time."

"I don't expect you to forgive me."

"Look, Kit." Meg grabbed Kit's arm. "I just want you to get better."

"Maybe my parents were right. They said I'd never amount to anything."

"They were wrong."

"Meg, aren't you angry? At me? Brad? What we did was despicable!"

"Kit, please . . ."

"No, damnit! Stop acting like Mother Theresa. You should be pissed as hell."

Meg rubbed her eyes and shook her head. "Yes, I'm angry. Okay? I'm damned angry. But I'm scared too. Of what's happening to you. To us."

"I'll call you, Meg."

Meg stepped forward to hug Kit good-bye, but Kit turned abruptly and walked away. Her image faded into the crowded corridor and was gone. Kit never looked back and Meg had headed for the exit.

After the airport, after the traffic jam, Meg

arrived at the big house to discover a strange car parked in the driveway. She opened the front door warily. Unfamiliar voices were coming from the living room. Maybe she'd left the TV on.

"Hello? Is someone here?" she called out.

The sound of approaching footsteps startled her. A few seconds later Michael Gregory stood in the living room doorway, a callous sneer plastered across his unshaven face. His lips broke into a broad grin quickly followed by a snide laugh. "Well, look who's here. My new roommate."

Meg stiffened. "I beg your pardon."

"Just moved in this afternoon. Sorry you weren't here to greet us. We took the back bedroom upstairs — although your room has a much better view."

"Who's we?"

Michael leaned back, yelling into the living room. "Sharon! Sharon, get in here. Meet my lovely sister! Hurry up!"

"You've got no business being here."

"Oh, but I do. Remember we're joint owners now." He smiled again, the kind of smile that could turn a stomach and probably had.

A timid-looking woman entered the room, taking her place at Michael's side. She was a thin brunette wearing skin-tight pink jeans, a white and black polka dot blouse tied into a knot at the waist and bright pink sneakers. If she hadn't known better, Meg could've sworn it was Annette Funicello minus the mouse ears.

"Honey, who's this?" she asked, eyelashes aflutter.

"It's my sister, Meg. We're going to be good friends — get to know each other after all these years."

Meg felt her face grow hot. "Not likely," she barked, stepping toward the phone.

"Call your lawyer if you want. There's nothing he can do about it. I have the court's permission. Care to check it out?"

Meg put the phone down and eyed the official-looking document as it floated across the table. It was a decree from the Nantucket District Court re-deeding the house to both she and Michael Gregory. "Why didn't I get a copy of this?"

"Beats me. Ask your lawyer."

"You bet I will. And I can assure you I won't be staying here."

"Fine. No sweat. Sharon and I'll continue to make ourselves at home. Visit whenever you like."

"There was no need to do this, Gregory. No need at all. This could've been settled pleasantly."

"Please. Call me Mike. After all, we're brother and sister."

"Maybe. But in this case, blood isn't thicker than water."

"C'mon. Don't be so moody. Sulking won't help. By the way, where's your friend? You know, the attractive quiet one. Quiet, like a woman should be." Michael looked at Sharon, shook his head and frowned.

"Visiting family in Florida."

"What a pity. Really wanted to get to know her better. Couldn't seem to find her room. Where does she sleep?"

"None of your business."

"This is a big house — room enough for everyone. But only one of the rooms upstairs looks lived in."

"Well, you found one for yourself, didn't you?"

"There were a lot to choose from." He smirked again, rubbing his hand across his bearded chin. Eyeing Meg up and down, he grimaced. "Oh, no. Don't tell me you're both queer. Shit. Just my luck. You two fuck each other."

"That's it, mister. I don't have to put up with any more shit from you."

"After all these years I find out my rich older sister's a queer. Christ. Well, you certainly have good taste in women."

Sharon's face twisted into a questioning expression. She leaned toward Michael and asked in a stage whisper, "Queer? Does that mean she sleeps with women?"

"Yes, dummy. For Christ's sake." Michael brushed Sharon to the side. "So, tell me. What do you lesbians do in bed anyway? Must be rough without the right equipment."

Looking at the short squat man in front of her, Meg laughed. "You ought to know. I'm out of here. And you'll be hearing from my lawyer."

"Hey, honey, I look forward to it. Listen, you pay me half of what this dump's worth, and I'll be outta your hair forever. Until then, you'll find us down at the beach enjoying the view."

Meg turned, an unpleasant snarl crossing her lips. "Be careful. I wouldn't want either one of you to drown. That'd be a tragedy I just couldn't live with."

CHAPTER SIX

Meg's new store in Provincetown was drawing a large tourist crowd for the grand opening. The beautiful July weather offered sunny skies and warm temperatures.

Waiting on customer after customer, Meg happily witnessed the emptying shelves. Carl also helped customers as Linda ran back and forth from the supply room, restocking the display areas.

"If this pace keeps up," Carl said in between sales, "we'll be out of everything by six o'clock."

"That's okay with me," Meg said, ringing up another order. Finally something was going right.

At exactly 5:59, one minute before closing, a final customer entered the otherwise empty shop. Meg froze as the short stocky man wandered to a nearby display area where he eyed several pieces. Picking one up, he walked toward the register.

"I'll take this one," Michael Gregory said. "Didn't know my sister was so talented."

"The shop is closed," Meg answered. "No more sales today."

"Now don't disappoint me, big sister. I deserve some respect. The kind I never got from our father. Or that jerk who was our grandfather."

"Jerk!" Meg leaned over the counter, face inches from the man in front of her. "He's the reason you're here, buster. He was the only one who cared what happened to you. Why, I'll never know!"

"Bullshit! He just enjoyed fucking my mother."

"What the hell are you talking about?" Meg stared at him.

"Man, you don't know much do you? My mother was damned popular with the men in this family. First, daddy. Then the old man. I loved Mom, but she had lousy taste in men."

Meg pointed toward the door. "Out. It's bad enough you and your friend are at the house. But this is my store and I'm not asking you to leave. I'm telling you."

There was a crash and the spray of broken pottery across the floor. "Oh, now look what you made me do. Must've slipped." Michael frowned, his hands clasped together. "What a shame. Nice piece of clay."

"That'll be a hundred and fifty dollars. You'll have to pay for the breakage."

"Tell you what, sis. Why don't you just deduct it from the one and a half million you owe me."

"Hey, what's going on?" Carl hurried into the room.

"Better get wise, sister," Michael said, backing toward the door. "I don't care for your attitude. Could get you into trouble."

Carl moved toward the retreating figure in the doorway. "Did you do that?" He gestured toward the littered floor.

"It's okay, Carl. The gentleman was just leaving. It was an accident."

Michael ran his fingers through his hair. Pointing toward Carl he said, "I better sell that man some life insurance. Hope you're paid up too, sister. You folks have a nice evening." Halfway out the door Michael yelled back, "By the way, if you let me fuck your girlfriend, I'll knock a thousand or two off what you owe me!" He laughed, a kind of shrieking howl, then slammed the door behind him.

Meg bowed her head over the counter. Somewhere, from deep within, she felt herself breaking apart, unable to fight against things she'd never known or wanted to know. It was not a history she'd forged for herself, but one others had left her, a nightmare begun thirty five years ago and now suddenly resurfacing in the form of a man who seemed bent on breaking her and taking whatever he could get his hands on, including her dignity.

Carl put his arm across her shoulders. "Who was that? Why didn't you let me throw him out?"

"He's gone now."

"Was that the guy who claims he's your brother?"

"Yes."

"Should've broken him in two and tossed him into the street."

"No need to make a bad situation worse."

"Meg, that guy's sadistic as hell. You should get a restraining order or something. For your own protection."

"It's over. I'm fine. Let's go uncork that champagne bottle. We had a successful day. Not even Michael Gregory can change that."

Ocean winds whipped across the *Emily's* deck, making it impossible for Susan Marks to light a cigarette. Meg watched Susan from the corner of her eye — vibrant moonlight catching the silver highlights in Susan's dark hair. Finally, in exasperation, Susan threw her arms into the air.

"Damn! Hey, Meg. Could you provide a little wind block?"

Meg obliged, her own hands encircling Susan's. The match lit, then flickered out instantly. "Try it again."

"Ah, what the hell. Must be a sign. Should give up smoking anyway." Susan stuffed the cigarettes into the pocket of her windbreaker. The unlit cigarette was still in her mouth, bobbing as she talked. "Ever sail to Martha's Vineyard?"

"Lots of times."

"At night?"

"Sure. Not a lot of traffic at this hour." Meg looked at her watch. It was a few minutes past eleven.

"Want to get a closer look at the house Michael Gregory was staying at before he moved to your place. Try to find out what his connection to Luis Raphael is. Could be important."

"I'll get you there."

Susan looked skyward, shaking her head. "Full moon. Too much light."

Meg cleared her throat, summoning the courage needed to say what she'd planned. "I want to come ashore with you. Go into the house."

Susan took the unlit cigarette out of her mouth. "Absolutely not. You're staying with the boat." Susan steadied her glance toward Meg and smiled. "Besides, having you nearby would be much too distracting."

"I've got a feeling that was a compliment, but I'm going to ignore it for now."

"Only for now?" Susan asked with a grin.

"Listen, I want to go ashore. Anything I can do to help nail Michael Gregory will be a tremendous pleasure."

Susan firmly clasped Meg's forearm. "Listen, you pay me to do the dangerous work. Let me do my job."

"I'm coming with you whether you like it or not."

"Mmmm. I was afraid you were going to say that. But technically, you're the boss." She shrugged.

"Yes, and I've got a score to settle with Mister Gregory."

Susan nodded. "No doubt. But tell me, how is it

you can be so difficult and so charming at the same time?"

"Never mind. Just tell me what we're looking for."

"I'll worry about the specifics. You can help keep watch." Susan looked toward an invisible horizon. "We get in and out as fast as we can."

A while later, they were nearing the Vineyard. The *Emily*'s engines cut out as Meg skirted a nearby reef. Years of experienced sailing helped her safely guide the boat about fifty yards from shore. At the last second Meg dimmed the small yacht's lights, leaving the two women in moonlit blackness.

Susan dropped anchor. "Brought your bathing suit, I hope."

"Thought we were taking the raft."

"Too much moonlight. We'll have to swim." Susan turned on her heel. "You can swim, can't you?"

Meg froze with fear. Yes, she knew how to swim. That wasn't the problem. She'd learned to swim in junior high school, in a beautiful Olympic-sized pool. But never in the ocean. Meg looked toward the black water. Closing her eyes, she took a deep breath. "I can't."

"Swim?"

"I can swim. But not in the ocean."

"You gotta be kidding."

"Do I look like I'm kidding?" Meg growled.

"Then stay here." Susan walked briskly across the deck toward a duffel bag full of equipment.

Meg summoned every ounce of courage. "No, I'm going. I'll take the raft."

"Meg, I told you, there's too much light."

"Not if I guide it toward those rocks." Meg pointed toward a shadowy area to her right.

Susan shrugged and looked at the two-man raft. "Okay, okay. I give up."

Ten minutes later they slipped quietly into the raft. Susan stuffed a plastic water-tight bag into the small space in front of her seat, the contents unknown to Meg, and began to row, her strong arms easily gliding the small boat toward shore. Cool water lapped against the sides of the raft, some of it spilling in and splashing Meg's arms and legs. Meg gulped each breath, her body rigid with dread, wondering how sturdy a nylon life raft could possibly be.

Above them, the moon's translucent beams lit the water with a spectral glow. In the distance Meg could barely make out the shape of a large house sitting on a rise above the shoreline.

Susan reached back and tapped Meg's arm. "We'll keep heading in that direction like you suggested. We can hide the raft along the rocks."

When they reached the shore Meg felt a sudden chill. The black water seemed alive with secrets. It was hiding something. Always hiding something. Meg glanced behind her. Had she made a mistake? She ached for the safety of the *Emily*.

Susan hopped out of the raft and tugged it roughly toward the beach. Quickly, she turned to take Meg's hand, pulling her onto the wet sand. On the beach, sheltered by the cover of rocks, they sat concentrating on the hilly terrain and planning their next moves.

There was a steep rise to the house and an open

area from the top of the hill to the first ground cover. Susan started up the hill and Meg followed. At the crest of the slope they began a snake-like crawl toward the line of shrubbery along the right side of the house. It was quiet, almost too quiet. Another chill suddenly moved through Meg, an ominous shiver that made her stop.

"You all right?" Susan whispered, looking over her shoulder.

"Yeah, fine. Let's keep going."

Alongside the house Susan stopped at the third window to their left, a window that accessed the basement.

"Looks like we can get in here," Susan whispered. "I've only seen the house from a distance through binoculars. There may be an alarm system. I'm going to check. Stay put till I get back."

Meg sat, wiping sweat from her forehead. This was crazy. Her entire life had turned into an existence she no longer recognized. She cursed herself for feigning bravery. Maybe Kit was right — she should stick to filling green stamp books. She sighed, leaning against the rough concrete of the house. Closing her eyes, she tried to think back to February. When everything seemed normal. When life was happily boring. Until her grandfather died and events careened out of control.

Meg felt a soft pressure on her shoulder.

"No falling asleep."

"Just thinking."

"Don't lie. You were praying."

"How did you know?"

Susan laughed softly. "Your face said it all."

While Meg observed, Susan cut the window glass,

then reached inside to unlatch it. The agile woman then disappeared inside the black hole. A few seconds passed. Nothing.

"Susan? Susan? Hey, what's going on?" Meg whispered.

A hand reached from inside the house. Meg grabbed its inviting warmth, sliding one leg over the window sill. Slithering the rest of her body into darkness, she dropped to the ground into Susan's arms.

"You okay?"

Clutching Susan's shoulders, Meg could feel Susan's breath on her neck. The closeness of her made her feel safe, secure. For a moment she considered never letting go. "I'm fine. Except I can't see a damned thing."

"Here."

An object was placed into Meg's hand. It was a small flashlight.

They located the bottom basement step. Susan climbed up first, Meg taking her usual place behind. On the ground floor they made several turns through shadowy rooms and down narrow hallways. Finally, Susan stopped in front of a closed door.

"From my observances, this was the room where Gregory and this Raphael guy spent a lot of time. It's our best hope of finding something useful," she whispered, her face so close Meg could almost admire its features in the blackness. "Keep watch outside the door. I'll do the rest."

"Sounds easy enough."

"If anything happens, point the flashlight inside the door. Then click it on and off."

"Hope that won't be necessary."

Susan extracted a small metal device from her top shirt pocket. It took only seconds for her to pick the lock. Then she was gone — into the blackness of the room.

Five minutes passed, maybe ten. Meg strained to hear. Twice she thought she heard a noise coming from somewhere in the blackness. Was it Susan inside the room? Someone upstairs? She wondered if the darkened house was having a laugh at her expense. Suddenly, she jumped. There was a creaking, shuffling sound overhead. A soft clicking. Definite movement down the hallway above. Meg flashed the light into the room where Susan had disappeared.

"What's up?" Susan asked, stooping on the opposite side of the door.

"Someone's coming. Maybe more than one person." Meg turned sharply. A low bark filtered down the stairway. One growl and then another. Running footsteps.

Susan grabbed Meg roughly, pulling her into the room. "Out the window!"

As they struggled to open the window an alarm sounded. Spotlights flared outside. More barking dogs — louder, closer. Before Meg could assimilate what was happening she found herself lying flat on the ground outside the window, her ankle throbbing.

"Damnit! I turned my ankle!"

Susan picked Meg up, then shoved her along the left side of the house. "C'mon. I know it hurts, but we've got to keep moving. Damned back-up alarm! Shit!"

Fighting the discomfort Meg broke into a run, desperately trying to keep pace with Susan. Pain shot through her leg. She bit her lip to keep from crying out. Somewhere behind them a door slammed — the sound of dogs coming into the open yard. Reaching the hill, Meg fell and rolled down the slope. There was sand in her hair, mouth, nose.

Struggling to her feet, Meg saw the water only a few yards away. Susan was already at the shore's edge, frantically waving her on. The water. Meg faltered. The thought of running into its blackness was too horrifying. Limping badly, she stopped and turned. Racing toward her was a blurred shadow, its eyes shining and white teeth flashing. A fraction of a second passed as the dog leapt from the darkness toward Meg's face. Raising her forearm, she blocked its advance — the animal's teeth ripping into her nylon jacket. The weight of the dog sent her falling backward. Her head hit the ground. For a brief second she saw a white flash illuminate the shoreline. Its brightness preceded the darkness Meg fell into — floating and bobbing into nothingness.

CHAPTER SEVEN

She felt a sensation of weightlessness, a kind of floating that moved her in and out of a dream. In the dream it was bright and warm, soothing and calm. She remembered her feet being pleasantly numb, arms crossed in front of her while the rest of her body floated along like it belonged to no one.

Her grandfather was there — floating in the dream with her. And she kept asking him, "Why, Papa? Why?" He looked at her, eyes filled with sympathy, lips moving but saying nothing. He stroked her forehead comfortingly, hugged her tightly to his chest.

And still she heard herself asking the same question: "Why, Papa? Why?" Whatever the reason, it was hopeless to keep on asking it. She couldn't hear a thing.

Finally, she began to drift off into another part of the dream. She heard a young girl crying, screaming out her name. "Meg! Meg! Help me!" Then the voice was gone and she heard another. It was a soothing voice like her grandfather's, but female. It came from somewhere above the warm floating. She followed it, trying to bring feeling back into a body that seemed to loll helplessly along like an old river log. A burst of warmth washed over her, the kind of warmth that came from the sun on a muggy August morning. Hot. Damp. Heavy. The warmth anchored her, flattened her into a more familiar dimension.

The voice above her was clearer now. Defined and strong. Yet comforting. And when she opened her eyes she saw its face. Lined with worry. Gray with fear.

"Meg, thank God you're awake. I was getting worried."

Meg felt a hand wrapped around her own. "Are we back on the boat?"

"Yes." Susan hung her head, her forehead deeply furrowed. "After I got you on board I drove the boat away from the reef. When I thought we were far enough from shore, I dropped anchor. It'll be light soon."

"The dog . . ."

Susan winced. "I had to shoot it. Damn!"

"I fell. I'm sorry."

Susan reached out and gently flipped the hair away from Meg's eyes. "We got away. That's the important thing..." Susan's voice trailed off. "It's my fault."

"No! I'm the one who insisted on going with you. If I hadn't been such a klutz and turned my ankle —"

"I let feelings get in the way of my job."

"Feelings?"

"I wanted so much to help you. I let those feelings interfere with my work."

"Don't you want to help all your clients?"

"Of course." Susan shoved her hands into her pockets. "Don't know what I would've done if anything terrible had happened to you."

"I'm okay. Really."

"Anything I can get you?"

"Don't think so."

"Your arm is fine, by the way. The dog ripped into your jacket, but luckily not into you. Also checked your ankle. It's swollen. I wrapped it in ice."

"I need to find out where we are." Meg struggled to a sitting position. Easing her legs over the side of the bed, she realized she was wearing a robe.

"Your clothes are hanging to dry." Susan smiled, a sheepish grin that broke through the hard exterior. "Actually, it was the highlight of the evening."

Meg laughed. "Glad you were having fun while I was unconscious and helpless."

Susan gently grabbed Meg's arm. "You were never helpless, Meg." Suddenly distracted, she walked quickly to the other side of the room. Gazing out the small circular window she said, "Yes, it'll be light soon."

"Please don't blame yourself for what happened."

Turning on her heels, Susan said firmly, "I *am* to

blame. I'm a professional, Meg. And I was caught unprepared because I had my mind on other things. I can't let that happen again."

"I'm sure you won't." Meg wasn't exactly sure what Susan was talking about, but she felt drawn to her, curious.

Susan returned to the bed. "I'm not so sure." Meg saw the face above her suddenly change. Softened. Sensitized. Susan sat down next to her. "Do you know the first rule of an investigator?"

"No."

"Never get involved with a client. I never have." Susan's strong arms molded themselves around Meg like the protective wrappings of bark around a solitary tree. "Until now." Susan nuzzled her face against Meg's neck. "It's been three years since I've felt like this. Everything was . . . dead inside."

Then Susan kissed her — the warmth of Susan's mouth making Meg's heart beat faster, her cheeks flush. She looked into Susan's silver-gray eyes. Fell into them. Long and hard — never hitting ground. Until she thought of Kit. And the thoughts stung. Kit and Brad. And the thoughts slammed. Susan. And the thoughts faded. Gone like a bad day. Pushed decisively away.

Suddenly Susan picked her up and laid her across the bed. Bending down to kiss her, Susan opened Meg's robe, and she felt hands on her breasts, her nipples hard. She could barely breathe. Clutching Susan's forearms, she tried to ground herself. Tried to reason with confusion. But another kiss took reason away. And that was reason enough to let go.

Susan began to remove her own clothes. Meg reached out to unbutton Susan's shirt, her hands slipping inside to caress the strong shoulders, muscled arms.

Susan's hands were everywhere. Loving caresses, lingering touches. "As soon as I met you, I knew."

"Knew?" she murmured.

"We were going to be lovers."

Meg unbuckled Susan's belt, pulled Susan's jeans below her hips. A few minutes later they were both unclothed, Susan lying on top of her, kissing her forehead, mouth, neck.

"Thank you for bringing me back to life," Susan whispered. "I've been gone a long time."

Meg ran her hands through Susan's hair — then traced the bridge of her nose with her fingertip. "I'm glad you're back."

Meg felt the graceful movement of Susan's body against her own. Lips around her nipples. Suddenly, another kiss — long and sensuous. Susan lowered herself and gently parted Meg's legs, her tongue's slow movements between Meg's thighs delicate and loving. Meg placed her hands over Susan's hands as they rested at her hips. Their fingers interlocked tightly as Meg's entire body ached for that final pleasure. Slowly, she shuddered over the top, again and again until she had to coax Susan upward. She laughed nervously, trying to stop the free fall away from herself.

Susan kissed her again, her teeth softly biting the outer edges of her bottom lip. "I don't think you're finished yet."

"Oh, God . . . I must be. I . . ."

Susan held her close, then parted her thighs and slipped inside. Meg followed the strong thrusts, moving her hips in a rhythm that became their own.

She clutched Susan tightly, straining to give access. To give up control. Surrendering herself. Giving everything. No longer afraid. Susan's tongue encircled Meg's breast, her hand moving deeper. Meg wrapped her legs around Susan's back, pressing her closer. She came again — expelling emotion as in some ritualistic exorcism. Loneliness. Abandonment. Anger. She drew two deep breaths and felt herself float into Susan's arms where, finally, there was something to hold on to.

Susan continued to kiss her neck, shoulders, fingertips. When she looked up into Susan's eyes she saw tears.

"Are you thinking of . . ." *Jan*, Meg wanted to say, but didn't.

"No," Susan answered quickly. "That's just it. I'm not."

Still floating, Meg closed her eyes. Encounters with Susan, like movie stills, flashed one by one through her mind. The darks and lights of unremarkable moments that had somehow led to intimacy.

"You're a fantastic woman, Meg Rhyland. I'm sure I'm not the first person to tell you that."

Meg kissed her mouth, rolling over on top of her. "As a matter of fact you are."

"I find that hard to believe."

"Right now, I find everything hard to believe."

CHAPTER EIGHT

The Provincetown club was jammed, clogged with bodies standing, sitting, dancing. Meg caught a glimpse of Hollis towering above the other women at the opposite end of the bar. Squeezing her way through the muggy room, Meg grabbed Hollis's arm and whispered a greeting in her ear, "Where've you been all my life?"

The large woman spun around. "Meg! Where the hell've you been? I've been callin' the boat, callin' the shop — and then I called the house and that creep Gregory answered! You okay?"

"Marginally."

"Carl and Linda said you took the day off. They seemed worried too."

"Needed time to think."

"I hear Kit left for Florida. What's that all about?"

Meg looked up at the ceiling. "Visiting her sister."

"And . . ."

"And . . . we've been having some problems."

"Crap! That sucks. Especially with everything you're already goin' through."

"I need a beer." Meg rubbed her eyelids with her thumb and the first two fingers of her hand. "Badly."

"No problem, sweetie." Hollis reached a long arm over the bar — grabbing and pulling the shirt of the bartender toward her. "Ted — quick. My friend here needs a drink."

The bartender put his hands on his hips. "Hollis, can't you be patient like everyone else?"

"This is an emergency. And I tip good, so hurry it up."

Freeing himself from Hollis's grasp, he removed a beer from the nearest cooler. "Okay, okay! Keep your pants on!"

Hollis glanced around the room filled with women. "That would be a waste."

Meg and Hollis found a corner in the back of the club where a group of women had recently abandoned their table. Hollis threw herself in front of the table as several other people rushed toward it. "Back, ladies, back. Better luck next time." Brushing the dirty glasses and empty beer bottles aside, Hollis sat across from Meg, gagging in the cloud of smoke. Hollis waved at the air. "People who smoke aren't the only ones who're gonna get cancer. Geez!"

"Face it Hol, we're all going to die."

"Yeah, sooner than we thought. Hey, how come you're limpin'? Hurt yourself?"

"Slight ankle sprain." Meg leaned toward her friend, trying to talk above the loud music without screaming. "Listen, Hol, things are really in a state of upheaval. Gregory's parked his ass out at the big house, Kit's gone to Florida, and Susan Marks is..."

"Is what?"

Meg looked down at the table, pressing her forehead onto the top of her beer bottle. "We...uh, last night, that is...Susan and I..."

"Aw, geez. Don't tell me you two did the wild thing! Meg!"

"Once, Hol. Only once. Shit!" Meg threw her arms up in the air. "I don't know what happened."

"What about what's gonna happen?"

"I'm confused. Really and truly confused. Maybe it was just a casual thing on her part — I don't know." Meg looked into her friend's eyes. "But I don't think so."

"What about you?"

Meg frowned. "Hol, I think you know me better than that. You're talking to someone who's been with the same woman for over four years, and never, never, not once..."

"Well, your streak's broken now."

"Speaking of Susan, here she comes."

Hollis looked over her shoulder. Weaving her way

through the crowd was the shapely investigator, dressed in a light chambray shirt and forest green slacks. Susan made her way toward the table. Hollis sat, her mouth wide open, then took a swig of beer, wiping her face with the back of her hand. "Shit. What a doll."

"Beautiful person too."

"How bad do you have it for her?"

"My knees are shaking."

"That bad?"

"Told her to meet us here."

Hollis sank her jaw into her hands. "The evenin's off and runnin'."

Susan smiled broadly as she reached the table. "Evening, ladies."

Meg took her hand. "Susan, this is my best friend, Hollis Shea."

Susan nodded politely. "Pleasure meeting you, Hollis."

"Heck, the pleasure's all mine." As Hollis reached out to shake Susan's hand, another patron bumped her from behind. Hollis's beer splashed across Susan's chest.

"Damn," Susan said, wiping the beer from her shirt.

"Here, let me help you," Hollis offered anxiously. "Please."

"It's okay, thanks." Susan glanced at Meg. "Can I sit?"

Meg slid one chair to the right. "Hollis works for the post office. She's a mail carrier."

"Ah, so you work for the government," Susan said, taking out a cigarette.

"In the loosest sense, yeah. They need a workhorse like me to keep 'em in business."

Susan tamped her cigarette on the table. "I used to work for the government."

Hollis sipped her beer. "Really?"

"Yeah, but we had a falling out. Long story."

Meg was silent while Susan and Hollis talked. She could feel the warmth of Susan next to her, the attraction of her presence only inches away. Out of the corner of her eye she watched Susan talk, saw her lips moving, the same lips that had kissed her passionately as the sun rose that morning. Still talking to Hollis, Susan turned slightly in her chair and placed a hand on Meg's thigh. Meg felt the soft pressure and her insides jumped. A tingling sensation shot from her stomach to her toes.

"Hey, Susan. Why don't I get you a beer? The service is a little slow tonight." Hollis got up from the table. "Meg, you want another?"

"Please." Meg watched her friend wander off, suddenly engulfed in a sea of bodies. Her protection had vanished. Protection from what?

Susan rested her arm along Meg's back. "Let's dance."

"You forget — I'm wounded." Meg pointed toward her ankle.

"Then let's go out to the dance floor and gaze into each other's eyes. We need to talk anyway."

Limping along behind the self-assured woman, Meg grimaced. The uneven gait made her feel like damaged goods.

Somewhere in her head the music died and Meg heard only the soft breathing of the woman whose arms were anchored securely around her waist. Someone strong. Steady and unafraid. Damn, this was what she needed right now.

Susan spoke softly into Meg's ear. "Developed the photos I took of some documents I found in Raphael's office. Seems Raphael runs an import-export business. What your brother's connection is to him, I still don't know. I'm running Raphael's name through the FBI AIDS network along with a print I lifted from his desk."

"AIDS network?"

"Not the disease. It's the Automated Identification Division System. Totally computerized. Can process information within twenty-four hours."

"What will that tell us?"

"Everything or nothing. But this import-export business has a bad smell to it. Possibly a front for something else. Something illegal. It's only guesswork right now." Susan pursed her lips. "There was something else too."

"What?"

"I found a strange military insignia patch that I'm also having the FBI check out. It wasn't one I recognized. For some reason it seemed important to me. I'm not exactly sure why. Just a hunch."

"I'm glad you're on my side."

Susan took Meg's arms and placed them around her neck. Kissing Meg's forehead, she said, "I'm on your side. My only concern is that working for you and loving you are things that need to be separate. And I'm not sure that's possible."

"Maybe not. I have complications of my own, Susan."

"Kit."

"I don't want anyone to get hurt."

Susan cupped Meg's face. "That may not be possible either."

"Will you stop by the boat tonight?"

"I've got to meet someone first. Business. Wait up for me?"

"Yes."

Meg read the same page twice before giving up. The plotless rambling narrative was really beginning to annoy her. She sighed, threw the book on the night table and pulled the cool sheets around her skin. She stole a look at the digital clock. One a.m. Suddenly, the lamp flickered and went out, leaving her in total darkness. The cabin lights in the next room were also out. Meg felt for the night light. She flipped the switch several times. Nothing.

Another generator problem at the docking office, she thought as she slipped into her robe. Looking out the nearby window, she expected to see the swell of waves that usually signaled an oncoming storm. But the water was calm and the sky bright with stars and the still-full moon. A problem with the *Emily*'s wiring, no doubt. Blown fuse. Faulty circuit breaker. Sliding her hands along the walls, Meg guided herself into the next room.

In the salon she stopped abruptly, noticing the shadow of a person standing at the bottom of the steps. A shadow barely visible in the moonlit room.

"Susan, you scared me. For God's sake." Meg sat down on a nearby chair. But the shadow didn't move. "Susan? You okay?"

The silence was broken by footsteps moving heavily forward. "Into the back room. Now!" It was a man's voice — cold, hard. Meg could hear his heavy breathing, smell the mustiness of his clothes. His arm swept forward, the glint of something passing near her face. A knife. "I said get into the back room. Now!"

Meg could barely stand. Her legs were heavy with fear. Slowly, she moved toward the bedroom. Every horrible thought she could possibly imagine shot through her brain.

"Hurry up, goddamnit!" the voice hissed.

In the bedroom Meg stood against the opposite wall, as far away from the skulking man as possible. But the shadow continued to close in until it was only a few inches away. One hand clutched her neck while the other held the knife no more than a half-inch from her eye. His breath stank of stale tobacco and whiskey. His face was unrecognizable. A stocking pulled over his head flattened his features into a grotesque mask.

"You been snooping around my friend's house. He sent me to tell you he doesn't ever want to see you around his house again. Understand?"

Words came haltingly from her throat. She could only gasp, "Don't . . . know . . . what . . . you . . . mean."

"Don't mess with me, girlie! I ain't in such a good mood tonight."

"Must . . . have . . . wrong . . . person. Wrong . . . boat."

"This could've been so easy, so nice. You be a good girl. Promise to keep away. I leave. But I can see it's going to be a long night."

Without another word Meg was flung violently

toward the bed, then thrown onto it with a crushing shove. The heaviness of his body was suddenly on top of her, the warmth of his stinking breath along her neck. The cold steel of the knife against her cheek. A hand fumbled at her robe. Kill me, she thought. Get it over with. He tugged the robe open, one huge knee and thigh on either side of her waist. His hand pressed around her throat again, cutting her breath into short gurgles that made her dizzy. He opened her robe down to her waist, exposing her breasts, the cold knife blade circling her nipple.

"Not bad. Let's see what else we got here."

Meg closed her eyes, preparing for the oncoming nightmare. Maybe she was dreaming. She'd wake up suddenly in a cold sweat, turn on a light and this man would be gone. She heard him unzip his pants. Her heart pounded. Then she heard footsteps on the deck above. Heard the upper cabin door open. She sensed the man rise and stiffen, his arm dropping to his side. In that one instant she gathered strength, bent her knee and shoved it into his groin with all her might. He let out a scream, moaned, then fell to the floor. Struggling halfway to his feet, he hissed, "Fucking bitch. You're dead now."

But a voice from the forward cabin distracted him. "Meg. Meg?"

The stocking-faced man leapt toward the doorway, shoving his way into the salon. Meg heard a skirmish, running footsteps, a door slamming. Voices yelled. Crawling under the bed, she huddled in the corner against the wall and waited.

Until a voice called to her again. "Meg, Meg. Jesus Christ! Are you okay? Where are you?"

"Under here."

A hand reached under the bed and she took it, sliding out along the floor into Brad's arms. "It's okay, Meg. He's gone. Chased him up to the docking office, but he got away."

She didn't speak. Tears came in a torrent she couldn't control.

The two strong arms held her close, Brad's hand caressing her head, her face. "It's okay, baby. It's okay."

Meg crossed her legs and sat on her hands, still shook from fear. "I thought you left."

"My trip was delayed. Besides, I needed to see you — to apologize." Brad sat down next to her. "What Kit and I did to you was unforgivable. We were drunk —"

"Let's not talk about it." Meg turned away.

"Meg, I'm sorry. Goddamnit, I'm so sorry. But I'm glad my trip was delayed . . . that I came here tonight. If I hadn't God only knows what would've happened." He reached out, taking her into his arms. "Whatever you may think of me now, I do love you, Meg. I've always loved you. Hurting you is the last thing on earth I want to do."

"It doesn't matter now."

"Who was that creep? What the hell's going on?"

"I don't know." She got up and walked toward the nearest window. Looking out she saw nothing but blackness, the surface of the water formless, menacing.

"What happened tonight — does it have anything to do with your grandfather's estate?"

Meg laughed, a chastising laugh meant only for herself. "Probably."

"Well, I'm going to talk to Gordon Meyers first thing in the morning. There's something really shitty going on here, and he better damn well do something about it!" Brad got up. He placed his arms around Meg's waist. "I heard about Gregory moving into the big house. He's obviously harassing you. Trying to scare you. Fucking idiot! We're going to do something about that too!"

"I'm thinking of just paying him off. I need to get on with my life."

"Don't you worry. Everything's going to be fine, Meg. Trust me."

"Everything can never be fine again."

CHAPTER NINE

It was early morning. Meg turned over, noting the dimly lit window. Since she'd been attacked on the *Emily*, the boat had been redocked at a new location. The warm August sun missed her bedroom window now, leaving the boat in total shadow until noon.

Three weeks had passed since the attack. Meg was still shaken — trying in vain to block it from her memory. Susan continued to investigate her case and had moved in with her, providing both protection and companionship.

The FBI's information sheet on Luis Raphael

turned out to be extensive. Raphael had once been in the business of illegal drug and weapons smuggling. His primary clients were South American drug cartels. But he'd served five years in Federal prison and was no longer on the FBI's list of active cases. His new import-export business appeared to be legitimate; his chief clients were China and Taiwan — mostly the importation of cheap clothing, toys and other goods. Michael Gregory's connection to him continued to be a mystery. Gregory wasn't known by the FBI or the Bureau of Alcohol, Tobacco and Firearms. And, for all Meg knew, he could still be her brother.

Susan had also obtained the original report from the Boston Police Department detailing the accident that had killed Meg's parents. The thirty-five-year old file included an eyewitness account from an anonymous individual who claimed the Rhyland's car was deliberately run off the road by a second vehicle. The witness was able to remember the last three digits of the license plate: 2-1-4. Because the witness had been a homeless alcoholic, his version of the accident was never investigated by police — one more aggravating twist to a case that now consumed Meg's life. There'd been no word from Kit.

A hand slid across Meg's waist, a strength of motion pulling her toward the body next to her. She could feel the warmth of Susan's skin against her own, softness of her hair brushing her neck.

"Good morning," Susan said, kissing Meg's cheek.

Meg lay her head on Susan's chest. "Morning."

* * * * *

The shower water streamed over Meg's head and face. Then Susan's arms were around her again, pulling Meg toward a kiss. The taste of running water and Susan's mouth mixed with her own. Warm and wet.

"God, you make me crazy," Susan said, her hands gently teasing Meg's breasts, her tongue running around the outside of Meg's lips. "You're so beautiful."

"I love you."

"Love you too, Meg."

Susan kissed her again, then moved down to lick the water from her nipples. She bent her head back, holding onto Susan's shoulders for support. Her knees buckled but Susan quickly knelt and pushed her up, her hands at Meg's waist, her head suddenly buried between Meg's thighs. Meg closed her eyes and held on tightly, her fingers clamped around Susan's upper arms. She floated to the top gradually, agonizingly, like a diver coming up for air — needing it, wanting it. The waves finally breaking over her, and then she sank to the shower floor, sobbing and shaking. Susan's arms around her back.

"Hey, hey. What's this?" Susan sat down next to her, water still flowing over them. She held Meg's head against her chest.

Meg choked, barely able to speak. "Sorry."

"It's okay, baby. You've been through a lot." Susan kissed the top of her head. "Sometimes I'm so stupid. It's my fault."

"No. It's just that I'm scared. Never felt this way before."

"Nor have I. At least not for a long time."

Meg continued to cry, holding Susan's arms around her. "I've been thinking about Kit."

"I know."

"I wonder what we'll do when she comes back."

"Take things one day at a time. Kit's ill. We can't make any hasty decisions. She's going to need you, Meg."

"Like I need you."

"We'll get through this. I promise."

"Let's go back to bed."

"We'll go back to bed so you can rest. I know you haven't been sleeping."

"Will you hold me?"

"Yes. Like I'm holding you now — tight against my heart."

A few days later Meg lounged above deck, soaking in the hot sun. Her mind drifted in and around the past. Thoughts of Kit clouded her heart. She'd tried to call the Florida number five or six times, but Kit's sister always answered, claiming Kit wasn't in.

She sighed, deciding to give it one more shot. She went below deck and dialed. "Sandy, let me talk to Kit. I know she's there."

"Kit's not here, Meg. And she doesn't want to talk to you. Let it be."

Meg paced the small cabin, trying to maintain her composure. "I'm not letting anything be."

"Look, Kit's enrolled in a treatment program down here. She's being counseled. She's getting the help she needs. The last thing I want is you messing with her head."

"I don't want to mess with her head. I just want to talk to her. To tell her I love her."

Meg heard Sandy sigh. "Kit knows you love her. That's part of the problem. Don't you get it?"

"Get what?"

"Kit's not gay, Meg. She made a mistake. Talking to you isn't going to help. Besides, she can't talk to anyone while she's in treatment. Not even me."

"I'm not going to stop calling."

"Look, Meg, when Kit's released I'll tell her you phoned. If she wants to return your call then, that's up to her."

Carl locked the cash register. "Slow day, Meg. But it'll pick up this weekend."

"Hope Linda had better luck in Provincetown."

Carl peered out the front window, then flipped the closed sign over. "You know, I swear the same guy's been sitting across the street in his car for at least a half-hour."

Meg looked outside. "What guy? Where?"

Carl pointed to the parking lot across the street.

Meg tried to comfort herself. "He's probably waiting for someone."

"Yes, but who?" Susan interjected. "I've been watching him too. Carl's very observant. The guy's actually been sitting out there for almost an hour."

Meg looked at Susan who'd taken a seat on the counter. "Who do you think it is?"

Susan frowned. "Not sure. Ready to go?"

"Once I get the cash receipts together we're finished for the day."

Susan hopped down from the counter and walked to the front door. "Mmmm. Now I don't see anyone."

"He was just there," Carl said, putting the receipts into a bank bag.

Meg forced a quick laugh. "Maybe he was waiting for someone. I think we're all paranoid."

As Susan continued her vigil, Meg scribbled out the deposit slip. Her paranoia had heightened ever since the attack on the boat. Every noise, every person passing on the street made her jumpy, nervous. "Carl, can you make the deposit tonight? I have some errands to run."

"Sure, Meg."

Susan took one last look outside, scrutinizing the street from one end to the other. "He's gone. I think we're safe," she said confidently.

" 'Night, Carl."

" 'Night, ladies. Be careful."

Meg and Susan left the shop. About ten minutes later, the car suddenly swerved off Polpis Road, down an embankment and onto the sand about a half mile up shore from the lighthouse.

"What the hell happened?" Susan asked.

"Must've blown a tire. The car just went haywire. You okay?"

"Yeah. You?"

"Think so."

They got out of the car. It didn't take long to

discover the problem. The front right tire was blown and completely shredded.

"Shit!" Meg kicked the tire. She was exhausted and not in the mood.

Susan took her arm. "Have a spare, hon? We may as well get to work."

"Yes. Damn!"

"Now, now. Keep a cool head. We'll have this baby fixed in no time."

Meg opened the trunk. As she lifted the lid she heard the squeal of tires from the road above. Car doors slammed. Susan was already crouched beside the car.

"Meg, get over here. We've got company. I think your blown tire was no accident."

They watched the brush alongside the road part as the weight of two men pushed through it. They didn't look friendly.

"Listen to me, Meg. And listen good. You make a run for it. Head for the lighthouse. Keep running and don't look back. Find a place to hide and stay there. Hear me?"

Meg grabbed her. "I'm not leaving you."

"This is no fucking time to argue. Go! Now!" Susan pulled her gun and ejected the clip. It was full. She snapped it back into place. "Meg, run! I mean it!"

Meg backed away from the car. Every instinct told her to stay, but the look on Susan's face countered that desire. It was the first time Meg had seen fear in Susan's eyes. Meg got up, breaking into a run along the brush that bordered the road. She heard gunfire and fell to the ground. Back on her feet, she dashed up a steep incline and down the other side.

Picking a point ahead, she ran toward it. The lighthouse. Its white tower, orange-cast glass, high cliff-base. The lighthouse. She didn't know why, but it was the last place on earth she wanted to go. Only the distant sound of gunfire kept her moving. The rippled sand reminded her of clay. She could almost feel the grooves against her hands, the tips of her fingers slipping across the sticky, malleable surface. The touch of her hands molding the clay into a permanent object. How long could she run? How long would the potter's wheel spin, clicking and clacking her mind toward the red-bricked image in the distance?

Over the last dune and onto the grass Meg stumbled until she reached the outer building, running along its side. A white picket fence guided her movements. Meg paused under cover of the building, her chest heaving as she gasped for air, perspiration rolling down her forehead.

Looking back, Meg was surprised to see one of the men following her about a hundred yards away. Something glistened in his hand. A gun? Behind her there was nothing but sand, the lighthouse the only cover for miles.

Meg ran into the back yard. Suddenly, amidst the tall grass and scrub, she saw the well, its outline barely visible to an unfamiliar eye. But she'd toured the lighthouse many times. Played there as a child. She ran toward the opening in the earth, grabbed the rope tied to the metal crank and lowered herself quickly into darkness. About two thirds of the way down Meg let go — the length of rope cut short from years of neglect. Hitting bottom she felt the shock of cold water, a twinge in her bad ankle. A few feet of wetness edged just above her knees. Instinctively she looked up, wondering if her plan would work. All she saw was the sky fading from pink to gray. Like the gray of Susan's eyes.

Darkness came and so did the cold. The sub-level well was damp, the water frigid despite the summer weather. Meg's knees and ankle ached, the pain in her joints boring through her like a dental drill. For what seemed like hours she stood, trapped and frightened, wondering what had happened to Susan, fearing the worst.

Above her the shadow of the rope dangled out of reach. She felt the surface of the interior structure. It was old and worn, some of the bricks broken or missing. The well was slowly falling into itself — disintegrating, self-destructing.

Putting her foot into one of the crevices of the well, Meg was able to step up toward the opening above. She found another hole, then another until she could finally stretch a hand near the rope. She snatched it, grasping it tightly.

Meg swung away from the wall, letting the rope hold her full weight. She held her breath. Slowly, she put one hand above the other and began to pull herself from the stale air. Several times she slipped, her hands damp from perspiration, her skin tearing open from the coarseness of the rope. Each time she steadied herself, finding a foothold in the wall. Finally, she pulled herself over the last edge, falling with a jarring thump onto the cool grass. Quick gasps burst from her lungs. The sweat from her face mixed with tears.

Meg staggered along the beach, her legs stiff and sore. The wind snapped at her face, whipping her cheeks raw. It was at least five miles to the *Emily* — up around the point and a few miles south. Exhausted, demoralized, almost unhinged, she put one foot in front of the other.

Meg found herself drawn to thoughts of Susan. Dear God, let her be alive, she prayed.

The mechanics of walking, coupled with fatigue, hypnotized her into a semi-conscious state. As she drifted further into her own mind, she saw flashes of a confused and bitter young girl. Unsure of who she really was. Fighting to gain an identity. Fighting loneliness. She had a vision of her grandfather, a man she loved, yet hardly knew. Work was his life — travel and long hours at the office. Meanwhile, she sat alone in a house much too big for a thirteen-year-old.

Who was her grandfather really? Did his secrets come as a complete surprise? For as much as she'd always felt his love, she'd always known his distance. In a closed-off study he spent many hours alone. Sudden business trips would last for weeks. Over quiet dinners with only the sound of clinking silverware, his silences were unnerving.

Did his silence come from the divorce? A divorce he refused to acknowledge or discuss? He hadn't initiated it or accepted the conclusion — his wife lost to another lover. Then, a son and daughter-in-law lost to a tragic accident — an accident never fully explained. Too many losses. Too much pain? Perhaps silence had become his refuge. Or his way of protecting her.

Reaching a bend in the shoreline, a mass of rocks began to take shape as waves rolled like thunder onto the beach. Weaving through the shadowy mound of stones, fatigue began to overpower her. Stumbling, she braced herself against the wall of rocks to keep from falling. In front of her was another shadow — but not of rocks. This shadow moved, reaching out to take her into its arms.

"Meg! Thank God you're all right! I was so worried about you!" Susan clutched her tightly. They fell to the ground — hugging, kissing, holding onto each other for dear life.

"Susan. I wondered if you were —"

"Dead? No, baby. Not me. We outsmarted those creeps. They slunk into the darkness — humiliated, I hope."

"Who were they?"

"Not sure. But we better get moving. They may still be nearby."

"We've got a long way to walk, Susan."

"Just a few hundred yards back from the direction you came."

"Toward the lighthouse? The car? Those men could be waiting for us."

"Not to the lighthouse. Under the lighthouse."

"You're not making sense." Meg sat down on the wet sand. "I'm tired."

"Meg, listen to me. The cliff that extends from the lighthouse — the one that drops off steeply toward the water. Know where I mean?"

"Yes." The cliff. She knew the cliff. Its shape, its crevices, its grayish-blue rocks. Indelible in her memory. Why? Too tired. "I know it, yes."

"Good. We're going to wade out about fifteen yards into the water and align ourselves with its westernmost face. At that point, we'll be walking on top of a shallow reef — it's only about three feet deep there." Susan stooped down, lifting Meg's chin toward her. "The reef drops off suddenly to a sheer underwater cliff-wall. About ten feet farther down, the wall splits into a tunnel. We follow the depression inward about twenty yards until the tunnel rises above water into caves below the lighthouse cliff."

Meg blinked and rubbed her eyes. "You're crazy."

"Trust me, Meg. I know what I'm doing."

Meg laughed at the insanity of it. "Now let me get this straight. You want me to go waltzing into the ocean, jump off the side of a reef and swim into some underwater tunnel? Is that pretty much it?"

"Yes. C'mon."

"No way. I'd rather get shot."

"You can do this, Meg. I know you can."

"I can't. Not in the ocean. I already told you that."

Susan stood, taking hold of Meg's shoulders, lifting her to her feet. "I'll help you. We can't go back to the car. It's too dangerous. And we can't wander around all night. We don't have much choice."

Meg looked toward the shoreline and the darkness of the water. The ocean. What had made her so frightened? A fear she remembered since childhood. What had held her back from its edges? Some hidden memory left untouched, a memory resting on the edge of her consciousness. But the more she reached, the more it faded away. "This is insane. But I'm too tired to argue."

Susan grabbed a dark object on the ground next to her. It was a flashlight. "Take my hand."

Meg trudged behind her as they paralleled the

shoreline. A few minutes later they reached the massive cliff below the lighthouse. Tightly gripping Meg's hand, Susan strode into the black water. Her heart galloping as she entered the water, Meg clenched her teeth so hard her jaw ached.

"Look, Meg. You've got to line up with that triangular rock dead center at the top of the cliff. See its outline?" Susan flashed the light, sweeping it quickly across the rock. "Now follow me." Susan sloshed through the water. "Just about here. This is where the reef drops. Hold onto my arm and don't let go."

Meg didn't respond. They slid below the surface of the water. Illumination from the flashlight created a murkiness that was eerily distracting. Meg fought her fear, praying she wouldn't pass out. As Susan pulled her along she pushed off from the rocky wall to her left. Down into the gloom. Down into herself where a sudden flash of memory overcame her. Fear had thrust it back into her conscious mind.

She could see it. It was a sunny day, a beautiful day painted with the pastels of early summer. Blue sky, green grass, yellow shirt of her best friend, Sissy. Meg was twelve years old. Sissy was fourteen and leader of the pack. Sissy's real name was Paige. But all the kids called her Sissy because she was anything but. Sissy was wild, loved adventure, dared the biggest dares, even fought with the boys her age and beat them. And she was Meg's first crush.

That day a group of their friends were hanging out at the lighthouse — smoking cigarettes and drinking beer — glad to be free of parents and school. Meg was feeling pretty heady, having provided the few cans of beer taken from the *Emily*'s refrigerator.

A few minutes later Meg heard Sissy calling. Meg spun around, shocked to see her friend standing out on the cliff, a stiff breeze blowing Sissy's pants flat against her legs.

"Sissy, get away from there!" Meg yelled. "You'll break your damned neck!"

"Don't be a such a sucker, Meg! Get out here. The view is beautiful!"

"No way!"

Sissy shot Meg her tongue and continued hopping, one foot after the other, until she reached the very edge of the precipice.

"Stupid. Really stupid," Meg muttered. But something inside told her to follow. At a much more cautious pace Meg mimicked her friend's path until she stood about ten feet away.

"Why, Meg Rhyland," Sissy said, her hands on her hips. "Never thought you had it in you."

"Knock it off, Sissy. We're going down to the beach now. You coming?"

"I can see the beach from here."

"You'll fall. It's really windy."

"Chicken?"

"No. I just don't think we should be up here. It's dangerous."

Sissy shook her head in exasperation. "Meg, are you going to be a coward all your life? I bet you sleep with the lights on at night."

"Do not!"

Sissy smirked. "Someday we'll sleep together — then you won't need the lights on."

Meg frowned. At the same time she felt something tickle the pit of her stomach. "Don't be an idiot."

"Ha! I've got your number, Rhyland. Someday, I'll

have a lot more." Sissy turned and took a final step forward.

In what seemed like slow motion Meg watched the outermost rock give way beneath her friend's foot. "Sissy! No!" She heard the crumble, then the scream as her friend disappeared over the ledge.

"Meg! Meg! Help me!"

Meg threw herself down to the ground and crawled toward what was left of the ledge, the sharp rocks cutting into her knees.

"Meg!"

She peered over the edge of rock — straight into Sissy's eyes. Her friend was hanging there clutching one solitary rock that jutted out from the sheer wall.

"Meg, help me! Don't let me fall!"

Meg swallowed hard. Her friend was too far down to reach. Panic. Heart racing. Quickly, she took off her jacket, wrapping one sleeve around her hand and arm. Then she threw the rest of the jacket over the ledge. The jacket hung over Sissy's head. Close enough for her to reach. "Sissy, grab the jacket. I'll pull you up."

"I can't!"

"You have to!"

"No! I'll fall!"

"Sissy, are you going to be a coward all your life? Grab the jacket!" Meg braced herself for her friend's weight. She looked behind her, calling to the others for help. But they were all standing near the lighthouse like mannequins, paralyzed with fear. She was alone. But that was nothing new. "Grab the jacket, Sissy!"

Meg watched as her friend's hand moved quickly from the crumbling ledge to the nylon jacket. The dead weight pulled Meg forward, rocks slicing into her forearms, elbows, legs. Then both of Sissy's hands were holding the jacket. Meg clenched her teeth, struggling with the weight. *Please, God. Let me be strong enough.* She pulled from her gut — pulled an inch, then another. She closed her eyes and leaned backward until she shook with the effort. Suddenly, the jacket pulled free. Meg heard the scream, then saw her friend crumple against the rocks below. Bouncing once, Sissy had disappeared into the ocean's swell, the blue-black water sucking the body under.

Meg kicked out toward Susan, trying to scream with the memory. She felt Susan's arms clutching her torso, wrestling Meg upward into a depression between the rocks. A few seconds later Susan dragged Meg onto solid ground, pulling her up the steady incline that rose above the water into a cavernous tunnel. Meg screamed again, pounding on Susan's arms and legs.

Susan grabbed Meg's shoulders and shook her hard. "Meg! It's okay. We're safe now." She knelt down and cradled Meg in her arms, rocking her back and forth. "Do you hear me? We're safe now."

Meg pushed away, rolling over to the other side of the tunnel. She lay her head on the cool, wet rocks. "Just go away. Leave me the hell alone."

"Meg, for God's sake . . ."

"I said go away."

Meg heard Susan's footsteps fade along the tunnel rock. A short time later an orange glow filled the huge cavern with light. Meg looked up and saw Susan's face, her eyes cat-like.

"C'mon, Meg. You can't lay there all night." She put her hand under Meg's arm.

Meg got up slowly, unwillingly. What was the point? She followed Susan into an anteroom filled with equipment. A two-way radio, diving suits, air tanks, flashlights, food and water, blankets — even a mattress.

"Do you live here?" Meg asked incredulously.

Susan handed her a blanket. "No. But in my line of work the location occasionally comes in handy."

Meg wrapped the blanket around her and sat down on the mattress. She was tired. Too tired to ask any more questions. Too tired to care about anything. She fell onto the mattress and into her own black ocean of sleep.

The next morning Meg was certain she'd had some kind of wild dream. She rubbed her eyes and stretched her body upward as far as she could reach. Looking around, she saw the gray stone walls lit by several torches. The caves. Spontaneously, the shock and anger of yesterday returned.

"Morning." Susan stood over her smiling. "Hungry?"

"Not really."

"Well, c'mon anyway." Susan held her hand out and Meg took it. The coffee smelled good. They ate in virtual silence until Susan finally spoke, her voice soft with emotion. "I'm sorry about yesterday. I know that bringing you here was terribly frightening. I was only thinking of those men — and that maybe they'd still be looking for us."

Meg shrugged. "Not your fault. You had good

reason. Sorry I yelled at you. Didn't know what I was saying."

"You remembered something."

"Yes." Meg shivered, then took a sip of coffee.

"What?"

"My best friend fell from those cliffs when I was twelve."

Susan stared at her. Several seconds passed. "Paige. Paige Murray."

Meg looked up, surprised. "How do you know about Paige?"

"Paige was in my ninth-grade homeroom." Susan moved next to Meg, pulling a corner of Meg's blanket over her legs. "Everyone knew Paige. And what happened to her. You were there the day she fell?"

"Yes."

"You were friends?"

"I loved her."

"Oh."

Meg closed her eyes, clenched her jaw. "And I wasn't just there. I was ten feet away. When she fell I threw her my jacket and tried to pull her back up. She couldn't hold on. I saw her fall. Saw my best friend die." Meg turned and looked at Susan. "That day, and the day my parents were killed, were the two worst days of my life." She hung her head, suddenly filled with guilt. "I'd forgotten about Paige — until now."

"Sometimes the mind protects us from painful memories. The shock of something that terrible . . ."

Meg took Susan's hand. "I'd known Paige since I was six. She was everything I wanted to be. Brave. Fearless. Outspoken. Always in touch with her feelings. When I turned twelve, just before she died, the world was still swirling around me. By then, Paige already had it in her hands."

Susan nodded. "I didn't know her nearly that well, but Paige certainly did speak her mind. I was never sure how much of it was false bravado."

"Some. Once I caught her collapsed in tears outside her house. She didn't speak to me for three weeks. Never did find out why she was crying." Meg sipped her coffee. "It's funny, yesterday I wouldn't have remembered that."

"Sorry I didn't know you then. In a way, Paige was very lucky. She knew you were someone special, I'm sure."

"She knew. Long before I did." Meg leaned over and kissed Susan's cheek. "By the way, I'm meeting with Gordon Meyers this afternoon. He's got the trust fund papers ready for me to sign."

"Stall him."

"I intend to. We still have some things to find out about Mister Gregory."

"We?"

"Uh, huh."

"Pluralities make me nervous."

"Face it. You're stuck with me. And I've got some old scores to settle — with both the living and the dead. No more secrets in the Rhyland family. Every skeleton's about to come out of its dingy closet."

"Well, I'm a little anxious myself to see what else you've got stuffed in there."

Meg smiled. Inside she was determined. "I don't care what we find out, Susan. If Michael Gregory's my brother, so be it. He can have his share of the estate and be on his way. But if he isn't, I want to know who he is and why he's trying to swindle me. And I want to find out who killed my parents."

"Then we've got a lot of work to do. Let's get to it. Just, please — leave the dangerous stuff to me."

"Oh, I've no intention of getting involved in any more serious sleuthing. One sprained ankle and a bump on the head were enough."

"Knocked some sense into you, huh?"

"We can only hope."

"I'm sorry the preparation of these papers has taken so long, Meg. Been working day and night to move things along. I've also had to deal with your friend, Brad Hanson, who's been on my back recently. As though I can do anything to change the law."

"Brad tends to be over-brotherly at times. He's an old friend."

Gordon Meyers grunted. He seemed to be in an unusually foul mood. "Well, if you'll just sign this document I'll authorize the transfer of your grandfather's trust fund into a distribution account. From that account two checks will be issued. One to you, one to Michael Gregory. What address would you like your check sent to? I know you've got a new docking address."

"I'm not interested in signing these papers today. Next week will be soon enough."

"Next week!" The veins from Gordon's neck bulged almost to bursting. His lips curled into an unpleasant snarl. "Look, I've been busting my butt to get these papers processed. Hanson's been hounding me. You've been hounding me. Now you don't want to sign them?"

"No."

"May I ask why?"

"I've got some other matters to attend to first."

Gordon sighed. "And what am I supposed to tell Mister Gregory when he calls asking for his money?"

"Tell him I hope he's enjoying the big house — and that he can stay another week."

CHAPTER TEN

Susan showed her investigator's license and signed in at the visitor's desk. Wearing a special security badge, she was escorted down the long hallway to Agent Kramer's office. He was on the phone. With a wave and a broad smile he motioned her into a chair in front of his desk. Susan sat down, pulling at the uncomfortable skirt — part of the dress suit she saved for rare occasions like this. Trying to cross her legs in a ladylike manner, she found it hard to believe that most women put up with this discomfort on a daily basis.

Jim Kramer hung up the phone. "Sue, it's great to see you!" He shot out from behind his desk and shook her hand warmly. "It's been a long time."

"Five years."

The agent sat on the edge of his desk. He looked uncomfortable, at a loss for words. He'd aged since she'd last seen him — his eyebrows and hair peppered with gray. "When we lost you we lost an excellent agent. That's the way I felt then. It's the way I feel now."

"I didn't have much choice. A lesbian agent wasn't on the FBI's most wanted list, you could say." Susan smiled through the pain. Jim did too. He'd been her only ally through the entire ordeal — the harassment, lawsuit, out-of-court settlement. "I'm surprised alarms didn't sound as I came through the door."

"If any good came of what happened to you, it's that most of the scum was cleaned out of here. But the agency still has its problems. I can't deny it."

"It's good to see you again."

"How's Jan?"

Susan swallowed hard. Jim didn't know. She'd already left the agency by then. "Jim, Jan died three years ago."

Jim's shoulders slumped; he was visibly shaken. "Sue, I'm so sorry. I had no idea."

"It's okay. I could've called you."

"Yeah. And I could've called you. Damn." Jim walked slowly to his chair. He sat down and rubbed his eyes. "That was one hell've a nice woman. I haven't forgotten the dinners she made us. The way she took care of us — like we were two kids."

"When we were half-starved and working on a case."

"Yeah. She had a way of lighting up a room, you know?" Jim looked up with a questioning expression as though Susan might've forgotten. "Just when I thought we'd crack from the pressure she'd make a joke or whip out one of those homemade desserts. Little things that gave me hope we'd survive another day."

"She was very fond of you, Jim."

"It worked both ways." Jim cleared his throat, fumbling through the papers on his desk. "Listen, after I got that insignia you sent me, I did some research. What I found concerned me."

"What kind symbol is it? Looks military, but I couldn't find it in any of the official references."

"Well, it took a lot of digging, and I'm still waiting for some more information from Washington." He put his glasses on and opened a file folder. "The insignia belongs to a paramilitary group called the Massachusetts Special Forces. Hence, the initials *MSF* on the patch. The group dates back to the mid-Fifties. Was started by some disgruntled Korean War veterans."

"Disgruntled?"

"Yeah. Former Rangers." He pulled out some more papers. "The Rangers were a highly trained branch of the Army specializing in guerrilla-type warfare. All had high-security clearances and were trained to infiltrate enemy-controlled territory. They were self-sufficient units — even had their own

145

medical doctors who went through the same rigorous training, including survival, night-fighting, hand-to-hand combat — you name it."

"And?"

"During the Korean War most of the Ranger units suffered severe casualties. When the war ended the Rangers were permanently deactivated. Most were discharged — sent home. For many of them the Army was their life." Jim slid the background sheet across his desk to her. "The Rangers were a very elite group — dating back to the seventeen-fifties. They fought in the French and Indian War, the Civil War. About six months after the Rangers were disbanded the Army formed the new Special Forces, the famous Green Berets. A lot of former Rangers were pretty upset. Some decided to form their own paramilitary groups. The most active was the MSF."

"Dangerous?"

"The MSF was. It was broken up in the early Sixties. They had quite a weapons cache, and some ideas about blowing up some government installations. They were not a happy bunch."

"The patch I found looked fairly new."

"It is. I had some of our lab technicians study the material and fibers. They're all new. Blends made within the last ten years."

"So the group's started up again?"

"Could be. As I said, I'm waiting for some more documents from Washington. There were some arrests made in the early Sixties. I was hoping to provide you with a list of names, in case any could be linked to the investigation you're working on. As soon as I get the list, you'll get it."

"I really appreciate your help, Jim."

"Anytime. Just be careful. These groups tend to be fanatical. Extremely dangerous. Unstable. Don't go poking your nose in too far, okay? At least wait until you hear from me."

"You may hear from me first. I think I'm on the trail of some information that may be of interest to the FBI."

"Call me, Sue."

"You and only you."

Standing on the forward deck of the *Emily*, Meg scanned the pier — a long line of sea-aged wood. Finally, she saw Susan striding toward the walkway that led to the boat. She seemed deep in thought, her face lined with the weight of serious reflection. But her face changed when the ghostly gray gaze fell on Meg. A vibrant smile, a friendly wave and quickening steps transformed her appearance.

"Hi, babe. Miss me?" Susan called up.

Meg took her hand, half-helping her from ramp to deck, half-wanting the touch, the connection. "Every second. Was the trip successful?"

"As a matter of fact, it was. Boston never gives up all of its secrets. But some."

Meg leaned against the outer cabin door. "I guess I should at least kiss you before asking questions."

"That'd be nice."

Meg rushed forward with a hug. As she kissed Susan she thought how nice it would be to get away for a while. Just the two of them. To forget everything. Then the kiss was over, its magic quickly evaporating into the failing light. The heaviness of the present returned, twisting Meg's mind toward business. "What exactly did you discover in Boston?"

"A warehouse belonging to Mister Raphael. I'm going to check it out."

"When?"

"Tomorrow night."

"Please be careful."

"I will. I also found out some information about that military patch from Raphael's house. It belongs to the Massachusetts Special Forces or MSF. A group of fanatics that was supposedly busted up in the early Sixties. Not sure what the connection to Raphael is."

"Be doubly careful."

Susan kissed her cheek. "I will."

A tug horn sounded mournfully across the harbor. Susan's ears pricked at every noise as she searched the darkness. The warehouse was a black blob in the distance. She unharnessed her backpack and pawed through its contents. Finally, she found what she was looking for. Strapping the cumbersome equipment over her head, she adjusted the night vision glasses so that the blackness changed into a defined world of heavy shadow and green-hued light. In the areas of light an eerie detail revealed a bizarre third dimension — not daylight, not darkness, but an eternal dusk.

Susan shimmied forward, her camouflage fatigues blending with the shrubbery. Everything looked clear. There were no visible cars. No signs of security personnel. At least on the outside. She took a deep breath and headed toward the warehouse.

With a heavy clank, the grappling hook landed on the roof. Susan pressed against the rough-bricked exterior. The wall scraped her cheek. Silently she stood, listening to the hum of the darkness and the pounding of her own heart. Then she began to climb.

The warehouse roof was gritty with dirt and small stones. She left her heavy pack behind and scurried toward the skylight located about ten yards ahead. The hinged windows were rusted with age. Forcing them open took only minutes. She flashed a light into the dark interior. Several layers of I-beam supports would enable her to rappel from one level to the next until she could drop safely to the concrete floor.

She prepared the rope and snapped the friction belt around her waist. Swinging down into the darkness, she landed solidly on the first beam. Clutching the steel beam beneath her, Susan briefly considered her present danger. But danger had always been her drug of choice. It brought excitement, a heightened sense of awareness and an incredible feeling of control. She felt all-powerful, as if she could fly from beam to beam without a rope, free-falling toward the voices below.

Voices. Susan flattened out. She heard the shuffling of footsteps, then saw five shadowy figures moving toward the east side of the building.

Susan felt the beam's dull edge pressing into her face, her sweat-drenched hands grasping the vertical support through a half-inch of aged dust. Suddenly, the warehouse lights flashed on — old dull bulbs that hung two levels below her. They illuminated the main floor. She remained in darkness.

Far below the group stopped. Poor lighting made the shadowy figures impossible to identify. They pointed and gestured in low mumbles and drones. Then a forklift screeched into motion from the west end of the warehouse and deposited a load of crates a few feet from the group.

Susan rose to a sitting position, straddling the beam. From her shoulder pack, she unhooked the camera loaded with high-speed film. Several moments later she could hear its clicks and whirs. She winced at the sounds. But the voices below continued monotonously, oblivious to the living shadow hanging from the beam above.

Maybe hours passed — or minutes. Susan lost all track of time. The click and whir of the camera had long stopped, but the figures below were still there, seemingly undeterred by time or a need for rest. Eyelids heavy with fatigue, Susan began to drift into a light sleep. As she often did when she was troubled, she dreamed of Jan. Thoughts of her brought peace and comfort.

They'd met in the parking lot of an Acme. Jan was loading her metallic gray Toyota Tercel with groceries. One of the paper bags ripped and a tomato rolled, stopping at the tip of Susan's sneaker.

"I believe this belongs to you," Susan said, looking into the stranger's walnut-brown eyes. Jan was wearing a red flannel shirt and jeans, her straight dark hair resting just above her shoulders. She was small in stature — about five-foot-three, Susan thought. Her face was lovely and delicate, like a flower just short of bloom. Jan smiled. Susan was hooked.

"Thank you," Jan said, bending over to snatch a grapefruit.

Susan stooped and helped Jan pick up the rest of the stray groceries. She felt an immediate attraction and wondered what to do. She had no idea who this lovely woman was, and no intention of letting her get away. Susan handed her a bar of soap. "Live nearby?"

"Yes. On Quincy Street. Near Widener Library."

Bingo, Susan thought ecstatically. "I live in Cambridge too. On Ellery Street. Only a few blocks away."

"Really? I just moved here two weeks ago. Jan Baker." Jan's hand was warm, soft.

"Susan Marks. Maybe we can have dinner some night — since you're new to the neighborhood, I mean."

"Oh, I'd like that. I'm from Connecticut, so I don't know too many people. My company relocated me." Jan laughed and shrugged. "Nothing like starting over. But at least I've got a job."

"And a new friend."

"Yes. I should throw my groceries around the parking lot more often."

After their first dinner together Susan was in love. Helplessly and hopelessly. It wasn't like her to lose control of her emotions. But the next time she saw Jan, it was clear the feelings were mutual.

Susan lost count of the dinners, the movies, the walks. The days passed like beautiful dreams in the night. Until one evening she and Jan sat on the sofa in Susan's house, involved in another endless conversation. It'd been so easy for them to talk, to communicate. Almost without thinking Susan reached out and touched Jan's lips, her words suddenly cut short by the contact. She took Jan into her arms, kissing her softly. She felt a rush, a seizure of desire that was almost frightening. If this wasn't love she'd simply gone mad. There was no other explanation.

Jan rested her head on Susan's chest. "We've got to talk."

"No more talk. I love you — you must know that."

"Yes. But I need to tell you something. Something I should've told you before . . . before . . ."

"Before what?"

"Before you fell in love with me."

"Then you should've told me in the parking lot at the Acme. I loved you instantly."

"Did you?"

"First time you smiled."

Jan looked up at her. "I love you too."

"Then what's there to talk about?"

"I had my right breast removed six months ago." Jan kissed Susan's arm. "Cancer. Chemotherapy — the whole bit."

The words stung. Susan felt physically sick. She turned Jan's face toward her own. "Just tell me you're okay."

"The doctors are hopeful — and so am I."

Susan held her close, burying her face in the soft skin of Jan's neck. "Thank God." She kissed Jan's cheek, smelled the lovely fragrance of her hair.

"We're going to go upstairs, aren't we?"

"In about five minutes."

"The scarring's not very pretty . . ."

Susan sighed. "My darling, you're the most beautiful woman I've ever met. Making love to you is going to be an absolute joy. Nothing about your body could possibly upset me. So long as you're well, and in my arms, that's all that matters."

"Do we have to wait the five minutes?"

"No."

In the late-day shadows of that room, love took over. Inner doubts died with a kiss; self-imposed loneliness ebbed away with each touch, each surrender. Jan's love was strong, the heat of it unexpected, as though she too had cast off unseen demons and was grabbing onto life.

Later, as Susan slipped her hand between Jan's thighs, she heard Jan whisper, "I never thought I'd find someone to love me again."

Looking into Jan's eyes, Susan continued her gentle thrusts. "You were wrong."

Jan arched her back, held onto Susan's shoulders and trembled. Susan kissed her softly, her hand still moving inside. Wet with passion, Jan shuddered again. She kissed Susan's neck, nibbled her earlobe. "Want to know a secret?" she asked.

"Yes."

"I wanted you weeks ago."

Susan smiled. "And you made me wait. Watched me squirm."

"Uh huh."

"Well, it was worth the wait."

"Love always is."

Susan woke up suddenly, a painful cramp tearing into her calf muscle. Shifting her weight on the beam, she reached back and tried to massage the leg. And that's when the rope that had been wrapped around her arm began to fall, the coiled weight of it unraveling toward the floor below. Susan thrust her hand out, barely catching the last yards of rope. It stopped, dangling about twenty feet above the group of voices.

She blinked, watching the nauseating swing of the rope, sweat dripping from her forehead onto the beam. The sweat mixed with dirt — like the fear mixed with the pain in her calf. But she steadied herself and grasped the rope with both hands. The voices started talking again. Pulling slowly, she watched the rope begin to rise from light into darkness.

A few minutes later the group below dispersed. The warehouse lights went out and Susan finally descended to the main floor. She moved cautiously, her feet sliding across the sandpaper-like concrete — dirt and oil-slicked from years of human traffic. In between the aisles of stacked crates she shuffled, hunched over like a wind-bent tree.

The crates were nailed shut, the wooden slats stamped, *Raphael International*. Susan stooped down and, using a small hammer, began to work the lid. By the time the last slat was pried loose her heart pounded. Standing up she peered inside, brushing away the packing straw. In disbelief she removed a small ceramic elephant. She cursed under her breath. Ceramic elephants? All this for ceramic elephants? Pulling out more of the small gray pachyderms, Susan grumbled. She felt foolish, defeated. Wonderful! She'd been risking her life for cheap knickknacks. But something made her look again. And then she saw them — the small notches at each corner of the crate bottom.

Shoving away the rest of the straw, Susan loosened the false bottom. "What've we got here?" she asked aloud, wrapping her hands around the cold, steel body of a large rifle. An AK-47. Raphael was back in business. If all the crates contained weapons, that meant there were thousands of them.

CHAPTER ELEVEN

Hollis blinked twice. Her nose crinkled, matching the wrinkles in her forehead. "You know, honey," she finally said, "if I'd known about all this family intrigue when I first met you, I don't think I'd have tried pickin' you up at that bar."

"Thanks, Hol. Guess you prefer women with less baggage." Meg chuckled.

"Well, that depends on how the baggage is distributed."

"Of course."

Hollis walked into the galley, returning a

half-minute later with another soda. "Everybody's family seems to have some dark secret."

"Even yours?"

"Hell, yeah."

"What?"

"In my family it's me."

"Bullshit."

"Listen kid, my father's a die-hard Catholic. Three masses a week. Teaches C.C.D. classes. Lesbians are not allowed."

Meg rested her head on Hollis's shoulder. "I suppose you never hear from him."

"My father?"

"Yes."

"Honey, I haven't heard from my family in about eight years. When my mother found out I was a lesbian, she did the rosary for three days nonstop. I do hear from my sister. And even she calls clandestinely. Collect — from a fuckin' phone booth. Got two nephews and a niece I've never met."

"Sometimes I just want to scream."

Hollis kissed Meg's cheek. "No. No screamin'. You're my family now. And my other good friends. Our community of people. It's more than enough."

"I love you, Hol. Be lost without you."

"I love you too."

"Hol, do you think I push people away?"

"Like Kit?"

"Yeah."

"Well, I guess you're the kinda person that needs to be in charge."

"How does that explain Susan?"

"Maybe you're tired of bein' in charge. Maybe you need someone to take care of you for a change."

"Could be."

"Susan's a good person. I can tell."

"Yes. She is."

The small kitchen was filled with the aroma of fresh-baked apple pie. Meg sipped her iced tea as the older woman moved from stove to counter to table. Even in her seventies she was still elegant. Her face was worn, but soft and lovely, her figure slim in polyester slacks and a sleeveless cotton blouse.

Beverly had never been a secret — at least not to Meg. She'd been her grandmother's lover and companion for twenty-six years. When her grandmother died of a stroke in 1980, her grandfather had escorted Beverly to and from the funeral. No outward bitterness. Just two people saying good-bye to someone they'd loved immeasurably.

"It's been so long, Meg. I'm thrilled to see you." Beverly set two dessert plates, forks and napkins on a tray.

"I've thought about you a lot."

"Oh, and I've thought about you, dear. How's Kit?"

Meg swallowed hard. "She's gone away, Beverly."

"Away? Where?"

"To visit her sister in Florida."

Beverly smiled. "How nice. But you must miss her terribly."

"She may not be coming back."

There was a look of shock. "But why?"

"Kit's ill. I mean, I think she's doing okay. But

I'm not sure. I can't get much information out of her sister. Sandy's never liked me much."

She carefully cut two slices of pie. "What will you do?"

Meg shrugged. "Wait. It's all I can do. At least until I resolve some other problems. Maybe you can help."

A hand reached out to pat Meg's arm. "How can I help you, dear?"

"Now that Papa's gone I'm confused about some things. Like the fact that I may have a half-brother I didn't know about."

Beverly closed her eyes. "Oh, Lord. It's been left to us." The eyes opened again. "We've outlived everyone, you and I. Long enough to share the pain of the past I'm afraid."

"Then you know."

"About Michael? Yes." She sat down next to Meg, the pie momentarily forgotten.

"What do you know about him?"

"Just his existence. Emmy told me about her grandson years ago. Very much in passing. There was a great deal of pain there, so I never pressed the issue. She never spoke about him again. And the few times I saw your grandfather after Emmy died — not a peep about the young man."

Meg squeezed some lemon into her iced tea. "Why didn't they tell me about him?"

"I honestly can't say, though I think it was wrong. You should've known. But —" She paused. "— it's a different world now."

Meg was puzzled. "What do you mean?"

"Emmy and I met in the Fifties. She was still married. When she left your grandfather for me — a woman — there was gossip and terrible talk. And gossip about your father too. His . . ."

"Affairs?"

"Yes. And a child out of marriage. Things like that aren't as volatile today. It was a different time then."

"But my grandfather accepted you."

"Eventually. At first, as you can well imagine, he was angry, hurt, embarrassed. But he loved your grandmother. She was the love of his life. Of mine. It was the one thing we had in common."

"What kind of man was he?"

"Extraordinary. A war hero. Much loved in the community. Successful in business. But maybe not so much in his personal life. I think that's why he protected you. Sheltered you. It may have been wrong, but it was done out of love."

"Is there anything else you can remember that might help me? About Michael? Grandpa?"

Beverly closed her eyes again. "I remember Emmy's obsession with the house. She loved that house. And your grandfather was a bit eccentric. Never threw anything out. Emmy was always going over there — getting rid of things. She said the house was a fire trap, with all his papers, trunks, archives."

Meg smiled. "He was a bit of a pack rat."

"Good Lord, yes." Beverly poured some more iced tea. "I remember a story about your grandfather's study. He never allowed Emmy or anyone else in that room. Kept the door locked."

"That room was always off limits."

"Well, once a year, Emmy — this is when they

were still married — insisted it be cleaned. She told me that there was a false bookcase. You know, one that had a secret opening behind it, or something like that. She found it by accident."

"Really?"

"Yes. She said it was crammed with papers, old newspaper clippings, legal documents."

"Maybe it still is."

"Well, it's certainly something to check."

"How did you and Grandma manage?"

"Manage?"

"To stay together for twenty-six years."

Beverly smiled. Tears welled in her eyes. "Love. Passion. Strength. We took care of each other. There was a lot of good in our lives. And pain. But the bottom line was always us. The only thing that ever defeated us was death. And even that's temporary. Someday, we'll be together again."

"I admire you both."

"And what about you, Meg? I sense there's a lot you're not telling me. A trait you inherited from your grandfather, no doubt?"

Meg couldn't help laughing. "Well, if you've got another hour I'll break precedent."

"Let's sit on the porch. It's a lovely day. We'll talk and get fat on apple pie."

The sunset over Boston Harbor cast a bronze glow across the roadway. The glow trickled down toward the horizon in a thousand hues of orange and gold. As Susan drove, Meg leaned into the headrest, enjoying the view. "Wish I knew where you were taking me," she said, watching the sky fade from bronze to purple to gray.

"Want you to meet someone important."

"But you're not going to tell me who."

"You'll find out soon enough."

"I was afraid you were going to say that."

A while later Susan had driven into a not-so-nice section of the city. In the failing light Meg noted the browns and grays of the row homes, cracked and uneven sidewalks, dirt where grass should be. There wasn't a kindly looking thing or face — no children playing, no neighbors chatting on a stoop. There was only a desolation that seemed permanent, inhuman. Finally, Susan stopped the car across the street from a corner bar. Its neon light blazed, *Shipyard Bar and Grill.*

"Where are we?" Meg asked, getting out of the car.

"Not far from the harbor. The neighborhood is mostly fishermen, shipyard workers, laborers."

"Are you thirsty?"

"The person we're meeting owns the place."

The door to the bar was propped open. Once inside Meg understood why. The large room was enveloped by a cloud of smoke. Through its veil Meg could barely make out the line of men two deep at the bar, their low-pitched, animated voices buzzing in her ears. She stayed close behind Susan as they made their way to the end of the bar.

"Well, what've we here? Can I help you two

lovely ladies?" The bartender smiled, a cigar stub stuck between yellowed teeth.

"Yes," Susan replied. "We're here to see Carla."

"Izzat right? And who can I say's callin'?"

"Susan Marks. She's expecting me."

"Take a load off. I'll see if I can find her."

Susan and Meg sat down at a nearby table. The warm and smoky air made Meg woozy.

"I know this is a futile question. But who's Carla?"

Susan lit a cigarette, seemingly intent on adding to Meg's discomfort. "Someone who can help us."

"Thanks for being so informative."

The bartender returned. "Carla'll be right out. Something to wet your whistle?"

Susan nodded. "A beer, thanks."

"You, miss?"

"Glass of ice water, please."

"Now there's a dangerous drink, if I do say."

Meg wiped sweat from her forehead. "It's hot in here."

"Sorry. The a.c.'s busted."

About five minutes later, a waitress approached the table with their drinks. She was older but incredibly attractive, almost voluptuous, with figure-eight curves. "You girls look thirsty," she said, placing the glasses in front of them. "I'm Carla. Which of you is Susan?"

"I am. Did you get the information I sent you?"

"I did," Carla replied. "Mind if I sit?"

Susan got up. "Please. Carla, this is Meg Rhyland. Meg, Carla Stewart."

"Nice to meet you," Meg said, taking a sip of water.

Flashing a breathtaking smile, Carla sat down next to Meg. She flipped her brown-red hair back with a hand thickened by hard work. "I'm happy to finally meet you, Meg." She glanced at Susan. "Were my directions hard to follow?"

"Not at all. Uh, perhaps I should make the more accurate introductions now. If that's all right with you, Carla."

"Okay."

Susan looked back and forth at both women. "Meg, Carla — I wanted you both to meet as soon as I discovered your connection to each other. Your histories are intertwined, to say the least. I thought we could clear up a very important matter. Especially important to Meg."

Carla crossed her shapely legs, her left thigh resting against Meg's. "I'd like very much to help." She turned, looking directly into Meg's eyes. "I knew your father. A long time ago — a lifetime ago. Sheila Gregory was my sister."

Meg's mouth fell open, her thoughts spinning into a past she'd never known. She was staring into the eyes of Michael Gregory's aunt — the proprietor of a bar along the Boston shoreline. God, she thought, what next?

Susan reached across the table to hold Meg's hand. "I know you're surprised, Meg. It took me a long time to find anyone from Sheila Gregory's family. When I found Carla and explained to her what was going on she wanted to help."

"My nephew, Mike, was your father's child, Meg."

Carla sighed, looking down at the table. "My sister really loved your father. She died a few years ago."

"I know about Michael. Found out from Beverly..." Meg stuttered. She pressed her fingers into each temple, the pounding already underway. "It was hard to accept — that this horrible man's my brother."

Susan interrupted. "No, Meg. Not the Michael Gregory you know."

"Meg, my nephew's dead. Mike died in 1988 of a rare blood disorder. He was only twenty-eight."

"I don't understand," Meg said, looking desperately at both women.

"The Michael Gregory you know is definitely an impostor," Susan continued matter-of-factly. "All of the legal papers your lawyer produced were once legitimately prepared and filed. But they're void now. Because the real Michael Gregory's dead."

"I can't believe this." Meg felt helpless. "I mean, if he's not Michael, then who is he?"

"Don't know yet," Susan answered. "But I will soon."

"What about Gordon Meyers? Does he know?"

"I think he may be involved, Meg. Either that, or incredibly stupid," Susan said.

"No more stupid than I've been." Meg wanted to cry.

Carla cleared her throat. "My sister was very close to your grandfather. He was so kind to both her and Mike. Your grandfather and Mike became good friends. He paid all of Mike's medical bills and made sure he got the best care when he was sick."

"Papa never told me any of this."

"I think he wanted to, dear," Carla said, putting her hand on Meg's arm. "But he didn't want to hurt you with pain that was old and then suddenly finished. He was devastated when Mike died. He'd lost his son, and then his grandson. I think he wanted to put the matter to rest. Besides, he still had you."

"And your sister."

"For a while. But they eventually parted ways. As friends, of course. They checked on each other over the years — right up until my sister died."

Meg looked into Carla's suntanned face. "Thanks for agreeing to meet with us. You've answered a lot of questions and saved me from losing my inheritance."

"Glad I could help. My sister felt indebted to your grandfather. Now, perhaps I've helped her repay that debt."

"You have, and it won't be forgotten. Thanks again."

Carla got up, stepping away from the table. "Can I get you girls anything else?"

Susan removed some money from her pocket. "No, thanks. We've got to get going."

"Please, put your money away," Carla insisted. "And whenever you're in the neighborhood stop by for a drink on the house."

"We will," Susan replied.

Carla walked toward the bar. "By the way, you two make a lovely couple."

"I think so," Susan answered, taking Meg's elbow. "Call you soon, Carla. We may still need your help."

"And you'll have it, of course." The attractive woman vanished into a cloud of smoke.

Amidst a sea of stares from men who clung only to their beers, Meg and Susan passed through the crowd and the half-open door into the neon shadows.

CHAPTER TWELVE

Meg lay in bed staring at the ceramic elephant Susan had retrieved from Raphael's warehouse. There was something funny about it. It was a cheap piece, made from a hollow mold and an inferior grade of ceramic. The glaze was too thick and the color uneven. "I can't figure this thing out," she said.

"What?" Susan asked, snuggling closer to Meg. "It's an elephant."

Meg looked at Susan and smiled sarcastically. "I know that."

"Just a joke, sweetie. What can't you figure out?"

"The construction. First of all, the balance is all wrong. I tried to stand this thing up and it kept falling forward onto its head."

"That's odd."

"A flaw in the mold, I guess. The other weird thing is the trunk. The body was made from a hollow mold, but the trunk is plugged. See?"

"So?"

"It doesn't make sense. The idea is to mass-manufacture these things as cheaply as possible. The plug is an extra step I don't understand. The trunk should be hollow — like the rest of it."

Susan sat straight up in bed. "Let me see that."

Meg handed her the elephant.

"Get some newspaper, will you, hon?"

Meg leaned over and grabbed what was left of the morning paper. Susan spread it out beneath her. With one quick movement she snapped off the elephant's trunk.

"Mmmm. The trunk is plugged on the inside too."

Meg shrugged. "Looks like the trunk was a separate piece that got stuck on last. Very strange."

"Maybe not."

"Huh?"

"Maybe it was manufactured this way for a reason." Susan got up and returned with a pocket knife. Slowly, she began to remove the material used to plug each end of the trunk. Once removed she tipped the trunk like a spout onto the newspaper. A white powder poured out.

"Something tells me that's not sugar," Meg said.

Susan dipped her forefinger into the powder, then

tasted it. "Nope. It's heroin. Pure heroin. Raphael's not only back in the weapons business, but the drug business too."

"Now what?"

"Another topic to add to my list when I meet with the FBI."

The phone rang and Meg jumped. "The FBI, perhaps?"

"Don't think so."

Meg answered the phone. The voice on the other end of the line was painfully familiar. Kit.

"Hi, Meg. Thought I'd better call. Guess you're pretty sore."

"Worried. I've been very worried."

"I'm okay. Really."

"Sandy hasn't been very cooperative."

"I know. She means well."

"I suppose."

"Finished the treatment program. Haven't had a drink in six weeks."

"That's wonderful, Kit. I'm so glad. You should be very proud."

"One day at a time. That's what they teach you."

"Sounds reasonable."

"How're you? Any word on the house? The estate?"

"Things are moving along. Nothing for you to worry about. You just concentrate on staying well."

"Listen, Meg. This isn't something I should discuss with you over the phone, but I've sold my interest in the restaurant up there. I've decided to stay in Florida. I really like it here."

A lump formed in Meg's throat. Words were impossible.

"I'll be visiting you to get some of my stuff. So, this isn't good-bye or anything. Just wanted you to know."

"Thanks for telling me. At least I can try to prepare myself."

There was a long pause. "Meg. I met someone. In the treatment program. She's a great person and we understand each other's problems."

"That's important. I'm happy for you." Thoughts were assaulting Meg's brain like a hundred flying Ping-Pong balls.

"Anyway, I miss you. That seems like a terrible thing to say after what I just told you. But I do."

"I miss you too. One question."

"Yes?"

"Does Sandy know about your new friend? She seems to think you've been living a lesbian lie."

"What?"

"You better talk to her. Tell her what you just told me. It may straighten out a few things."

"I'll talk to her."

"Good. I was worried you might end up a prisoner in your sister's house for the rest of your life."

"Oh, no. I'm getting my own apartment. Circled a few places to look at this morning."

"Hope you find something nice."

"Nothing as beautiful as the big house, but I'll be okay."

"Well, let me know when you'll be visiting. I'll help you get your things together."

"I will. Thanks, Meg."

"Anytime."

Meg hung up the phone, slid under the covers and cried.

The darkroom was her isolation — her escape to private thoughts. As much as photography had become a part of her investigative work, it had also become a hobby. Susan looked around the small room. Aside from the necessary equipment — enlarger, chemicals, trays, tongs, film reels and other supplies — she had a sort of private gallery of black-and-white prints hung across four walls. Photographs of the island, family, friends and lovers.

The portraits of Jan still overpowered her. In each photograph, frozen in time, she'd captured one by one the sparks that had been the fire of that woman. A quirky grin that would suddenly burst into a vibrant smile. A shapely figure lost in an oversized flannel shirt. Night-dark hair blown across pale cheeks. Soft slim-fingered hands held in her own during long walks. There, on the darkroom wall, Jan was still alive. At times her presence was so strong Susan was sure she felt Jan's hand on her shoulder. A comforting pressure slipping through the cracks of another dimension.

Susan flipped off the light switch. The safety bulb automatically went on, its soft glow an eerie Halloween-pumpkin orange. Susan put the first exposed print into the developer. She'd sent the high-speed film to a special lab. They'd developed the negatives. Now she would develop the prints taken at the warehouse only days ago.

After a few seconds the images in the tray began to appear. As the shadows deepened Susan moved the print into the stop bath. Acid. A small concentration. Knew she should've worn gloves. But as usual, she hadn't.

The first print went into the fixer for ten minutes. In the meantime she started on the next. When they were all hanging to dry she turned on the lights. To study them she'd have to wait until they dried. The grainy prints would be almost impossible to read while still wet.

She left the small room and sat in the overstuffed chair outside the door. Lighting a cigarette, she thought about the past four months — meeting Meg, investigating Meg's life, its mysteries and still-unanswered questions. Was it the mystery she loved, or the woman? Meg and Jan were different in many ways. Meg was stronger, more independent. Yet somehow vulnerable. Especially now. But what would happen when the questions about her life were answered? When the puzzle pieces finally fit? When there was clarity and resolution? Would Meg still need her? Still want her? Susan was used to taking care of people. What was it that Jan always said? "Why me, Susan? I'm sick — I drag you down. I sap your strength. You could have anyone."

They'd had the same conversation so many times. "When I fell in love with you I didn't know you were sick," Susan would say.

"It's not too late to bow out. Believe me, I'd understand. I was dishonest. Should've told you right away."

"I love you, damnit. It's not that easy."

"You're a giver."

"A what?"

"A giver. Someone who thrives on holding other people up. Unlike me. I'm a taker. I take whatever I can get."

"No, you're an amateur psychologist who doesn't know when to keep quiet," Susan would tease.

"Is that a polite way of telling me to shut up?"

"Yes. Then maybe I can kiss you. It's the only way I know to keep you quiet." And they would kiss.

Susan flicked the ashes off her cigarette. Just as she'd admired Jan's courage, she also admired Meg's. In order to finally put the past to rest Meg had finally realized the need to face its secrets and mysteries. Good or bad, the information would be a completion of Meg's self and a coming to terms with those she loved. In that way, she could finally say good-bye to the demons and nightmares she still harbored.

In her own heart Susan knew she needed to do the same. For three years she'd defied Jan's final wishes. At times she could almost feel Jan's anger, as if it were alive, moving with her through the house. Admonishing her, scolding her. But the time had come to finally face what was ended, in order to embrace what was begun.

She stared into space and remembered one of their last coherent conversations. She had gone into the bedroom and propped up the pillows on Jan's bed.

"You have what I can never have," Jan said.

The chair seemed to weigh a ton as Susan slid it closer to the bed. "What's that?"

"Time."

"Time? I never have enough time. You work me too damned hard."

Jan smiled weakly. "You know what I mean."

Susan felt a sudden attack of nausea. "If I could, I'd give you some of mine."

"But you can't. So here's the deal." Jan closed her eyes, taking a deep breath through her nose where the oxygen tube hung, a flimsy plastic lifeline. "Don't waste it. Okay? That's all I ask."

"I don't know what you mean."

"God, Susan, sometimes you're so dense. Don't waste *time* . . . mourning or something stupid like that. Go on with your life. Meet a beautiful woman. Take a trip around the world. Make love on a Hawaiian beach. Sip wine by candlelight. Get a dog. A cat even. Buy a cozy house by the ocean."

"That shouldn't be too hard on an island."

Jan managed a smile. "Well, you know what I mean."

Susan squeezed Jan's hand. Her voice choked. "Those were all the things I wanted to do with you."

Jan snapped, "Well, you can't. And that's that." Her voice was hard. "Now go have a cigarette — and then I'll share some of my oxygen with you."

"Bitch," Susan said softly.

"Shithead. Now go. I need to rest." And she'd closed her eyes to nap.

Susan took a final puff of her cigarette. The last cigarette she would ever smoke. It was time.

She went back into the darkroom. The prints were dry. She carried the stack to a nearby table lit by high-intensity bulbs. Flipping the switch, Susan studied the first few prints underneath the bright lights. They were blurred and fuzzy. Not enough detail. The next print was clearer. She grabbed a magnifying glass out of the supply drawer and she concentrated on the five individuals she'd seen in the warehouse that night. Three of them had their backs turned to the camera. The other two had visible faces — faces that became clearer when magnified.

"Oh, dear God," she said aloud. "Oh, dear God."

The big house was deserted. Michael Gregory and his girlfriend were nowhere to be found. Two patrol cars were discreetly parked at the perimeter of the property. Meg had contacted them the day before. The police — and by this time, thanks to Susan, the FBI — were definitely interested in talking to Mister Gregory, or whoever he really was.

"Well, they left some of their stuff," Hollis said. "And they sure made a mess of the place."

In the kitchen Meg tripped over a dirty pile of laundry. The sink was overflowing with dishes. "Christ! The place'll have to be fumigated."

"At least if they come back, they'll find a surprise waiting for them. The police."

"Yeah. I'd kind of like to see that." Meg turned the corner to her grandfather's study. It was a room she'd only entered once since he died. It was a sanctuary, a memorial. Something to be left undisturbed. She turned the key in the lock and opened the door. Everything in it had been left untouched.

Eerily, as she stood within the entranceway, she felt his spirit.

"Wow. I've never seen this room before," Hollis said, wide-eyed. "It smells like your grandfather. Pipe tobacco. Old books."

"Well, let's see if Beverly was right. We're looking for a false bookcase."

"Cool! Like an Agatha Christie novel."

"Hol, for God's sake."

"Seriously. She wrote about a million books, you know. Lots of mysteries with secret rooms, disappearin' floors, hidden staircases."

"This is my life we're talking about, Hol. Not some paperback book you carry around in your back pocket."

One after the other, Hollis started pulling books out of their slots in the bookcase on the far wall.

"Hol, what the hell are you doing?"

"That's how it works. You pull a book out and the whole wall opens up."

Meg smacked her forehead with her hand. "Hol, sometimes you drive me nuts. Really you do."

"You never listen to me, kid. I know what I'm talkin' about."

While Hollis continued pulling books Meg concentrated on the shelf behind her grandfather's desk. She tried to move the bookcase out from the wall, but it was either too heavy, or built-in. She checked all the bookshelves — even her grandfather's desk thinking Beverly may have remembered the story incorrectly. Then she heard Hollis laugh.

"Ha! Thanks, Aggie. C'mere, kid."

Meg stood next to Hollis. She couldn't believe her eyes. Sure enough, Hollis had moved the first book on the third shelf. The book was really a lever — carved out of wood and painted to look like a real book. When the lever clicked outward it released the shelf, which opened into a hidden space about three feet wide and two feet deep.

"I'll be damned."

"What'd I tell you? You really oughta read more, Meg. Then you'd learn some of this stuff."

"I'll take that under advisement."

The concealed space was filled with more books. Upon closer inspection, the books turned out to be journals written in her grandfather's own hand. One journal for each year, beginning in 1945, right after the war. The journals ended thirty years later in 1975.

"It's your grandfather's whole life, Meg."

"Practically."

"I'll bet this stuff is really interestin'."

"That's what I'm hoping." Meg piled the journals on the floor and began to sift through them. She also gave Hollis a pile to read.

"What am I lookin' for?"

"I'm not sure."

An hour later they were both still reading. Hollis was lying on her stomach on the floor. Meg sat at her grandfather's desk reading the journal from 1961, the year her father and mother died. On March 17, 1961, about a month before her parents' death, Meg discovered an intriguing entry. "Listen to this, Hol." She read aloud. " 'Jim' — that was my dad — 'quit the MSF. Their plans disturbed him. Stockpiling of weapons. Pistols, rifles, explosives. Finally caught on to the brainwashing and rhetoric. According to Jim, the MSF was originally formed to protect the United States from communist and Fascist infiltration. They held meetings, recruited new members, participated in limited field exercises. Suddenly, the focus of the group changed. Our own government has become the primary target. The group's leader claims the government is becoming too invasive, too controlling. I fear this group. Glad Jim's left them. He's thinking of contacting the police. Thinks the group is planning something dangerous or illegal. He's not sure, but feels an investigation should be conducted.' "

"That sounds pretty scary, Meg."

"Susan told me about the MSF. She found one of these at Raphael's house." Meg held up an old patch that had been stuck between pages. The patch depicted a crossed sword and rifle. Underneath the emblem were the initials *MSF*.

Meg flipped the pages. A month later, the day of her parents' death, she came across another entry. " 'Jim and Emily killed early this morning. Police say it was an accident. Not so sure — but have no proof. MSF currently under investigation. Weapons, explosives confiscated. Revenge?' "

"Hey, Meg, they're a bunch of pictures stuck in the back of this book. One's an old newspaper clippin'. Say, isn't this your lawyer? Gordon C. Meyers?"

Meg sat down on the floor next to Hollis. The clipping included a picture of Gordon Meyers and her grandfather. The two men were standing at the back of an old Chevy. The caption beneath the photograph read, "10th Annual Nantucket Antique Car Show organizers, Richard P. Rhyland, President of the Nantucket Chamber of Commerce, and Gordon C. Meyers, 1980 Show Chairman, take time out to admire Meyers' classic '55 Chevy. This year's show will feature more than 1000 antique class automobiles."

"Nice photo of your grandfather. Heck of a car too."

"A beauty." Meg slid the clipping back into the book. Suddenly, a chill ran down her spine. The image of the photograph flashed again in her mind, registering something she'd not immediately noticed. The car in the photograph. The car belonging to Gordon. Meg opened the book and grabbed the old clipping again to be certain. But the numbers were there, plainly recorded in time. *2-1-4.* The last three digits of the car's license plate. The same car that forced her mother and father from the road. It belonged to her lawyer. "Hol, remember when you asked me about Meyers. Was he a good lawyer?"

"Yeah."

"Well, he's good all right. Good enough to fool me — not that it's been that difficult. Damn! He's involved. More involved than Susan ever thought."

"Hello, ladies. What's with the patrol cars?"

Meg looked up. It was Brad. "Brad! What're you doing here?"

He shrugged. "My schedule changes quickly. Thought I'd stop by for a visit. Wasn't sure who I'd find here. Glad it's you and not Gregory."

"That's who the police are waiting for. They've got a few questions to ask him. About extortion."

"Really? What the hell's going on?"

Meg dragged Brad into the living room. For the next ten minutes she explained about the real Michael Gregory's death and the possible involvement of her lawyer in both the scheme and her parents' car wreck.

Brad let out a long slow whistle. "Wow! I'm giving up travel. I miss all the good stuff." He got up from the sofa and started to pace. "You know, I'm a little worried about your being here. If he returns, and there's trouble with the police, I'm not sure I want you two in the middle of a shoot-out or something. Maybe we should go to the boat and wait it out. I think it's safer. Gregory doesn't know where the boat's docked."

Meg nodded. "Need to contact Susan anyway. She may be at the boat. Don't know."

Hollis looked out the front window. "Well, getting out of here does seem like a good idea. That guy Gregory gives me the creeps. He's dangerous. Suppose he slips by the police?"

Meg got up. "I'll just grab a few of Papa's journals. Then we're out of here."

Once aboard the *Emily,* Brad asked to speak to Meg privately. They walked out onto the deck; it was sunny and hot.

"Meg, as unbelievable as it is to me, I agree with your assessment of Gordon Meyers. I've been doing some investigating myself — especially after what happened to you on this boat." Brad began to pace, his T-shirt flapping in the breeze. He hugged a manila envelope to his chest. "I got suspicious of Meyers when I visited his office recently. I think your best interests are not his best interests, if you know what I mean." He removed some papers from the envelope. "That's why I had a very good friend of mine — a European lawyer, top-notch in estate law — draw up these papers. They authorize the transfer of your grandfather's trust fund to a foreign bank account — one that's safe. All you have to do is sign, Meg, and no one can take what's yours."

Meg was puzzled. "I didn't sign the papers Meyers prepared. Everything should be safe where it is."

Brad grabbed her by the shoulders. "Meg, haven't you ever heard of moving money electronically? I think that's what Gregory and Meyers are planning to do now that you've refused to cooperate."

"Those bastards."

"Listen, if you let me set this up your worries will be over. As soon as these two jerks are in custody, you can transfer everything back to your own account. But while these guys are on the loose your inheritance is still in jeopardy."

She clasped his arms. "Well, I'm not the financial wizard you are. I don't travel all over the world. Whatever you think's best." Looking at the strong arms that reached out to comfort her, Meg said a silent thank you for his friendship and vigilance. Then she noticed the tattoo on Brad's upper arm — the bottom half of it showing beneath his T-shirt. The butt of a rifle, the hilt of a sword. Underneath, the letters *MSF*.

She stepped back. Short of breath, she could

barely speak. "How long have you and Meyers been plotting this extortion, Brad? Months? Years?"

"Meg, what the hell are you talking about?"

"What's the money for? To buy more illegal weapons? Ship more drugs?"

He tried to grab her arm. "Meg, cut it out. You're scaring me."

"I know all about the Massachusetts Special Forces. It's the group that killed my father. You and Meyers must both be members."

"Now listen, Meg." He took a few steps forward.

"Don't you come near me, you son of a bitch! Stay the hell away!" Meg could feel herself breaking apart, betrayed and hurt. It was a final indignation she could hardly bear. No one to trust. No family left. Hatred pounded at her temples. Panic seized her heart. And an incredible loathing for the man she thought was her friend. She screamed.

Hollis ran out onto the deck. "What the hell's goin' on here? Meg, what happened? You okay?"

"Tell her, Brad — or shall I?"

"That's enough, Meg."

"You bastard! It was you all along. You're the one who masterminded this extortion plot. For weapons and drug smuggling. To raise money for what? The MSF? Has it started up again? God, how stupid I've been. Michael Gregory — or whoever the hell he is — and Meyers are working for you! Well, you can take your goddamned papers and shove them! I'm not signing anything."

Brad pulled a gun from the waistband of his jeans. "Hollis, no trouble from you. I'm going to have to lock you below. Then Meg'll pilot the boat. We're all taking a little trip."

183

"I'm not piloting this fucking boat anywhere!"

"I'm afraid you are." He aimed the gun at Hollis. "And you *will* sign the papers, Meg. I'd hate to see anyone get hurt. Hurt bad."

Meg guided the *Emily* over open water. Her mind ran through the last six months, adding up the pieces of a puzzle that finally ended with Brad. She wanted to rip his heart out — like he'd ripped hers. She wanted to scream again. But there was no one to hear her. She felt violated. Lost. Finally defeated.

"How long have you been running the MSF, Brad?"

"Fifteen years."

"Why? Just give me some earthly reason why?"

He laughed — a nervous laugh that stuck in his throat. "I never wanted to hurt you, Meg. Honest." He leaned against the railing, his boyish grin suddenly smug. "Once it got started again the MSF was a disjointed group for the first five years or so. Then I took full control. I broadened our goals beyond the occasional target practice and war games. I started to run the MSF the way my father had run it. To stop government from intruding into our lives and our freedoms."

"Your father?"

"That's right. He took over the MSF in nineteen fifty-seven when he was thirty. But because of your traitorous father, he ended up in jail for nine years. The government charged him with sedition! They didn't understand. He was a patriot. His vision of the MSF became a prototype for similar groups today."

Brad grew more agitated, his arms flailing, his gaze burning into hers. "So he rotted in jail. By the time he got out he was a broken man. He was only fifty when he died."

"You told me your father and mother were divorced, that your dad lived in Europe."

"I told you what my mother told me. They were divorced. When I never heard from my father, I figured he didn't give a damn about me. I didn't know he was in prison." Brad started to pace. "But don't you see, Meg? He was right. He was a man ahead of his time. The real enemy is the government. Much more so today. The FBI, ATF, CIA. They don't work for us, Meg. They want to take away our rights — our right to bear arms and protect ourselves."

"You're not making any sense."

"Seems we both take after our fathers."

"Bullshit! You're nothing but a drug dealer and weapons smuggler. Whose this stuff going to anyway?"

"Some friends in South and Central America."

"Raphael?"

"He's our lead negotiator, you could say. We've been trading weapons for drugs for the past two years. We sell the drugs in this country so we can continue to finance our training programs and recruitment efforts. Support other organizations that share our beliefs, that share our goal to free this country again."

"Fucking ludicrous!"

He shook his head. "You don't understand. When I came back from Vietnam I was a changed man. Over there I found out how much our country and government had deteriorated. It was sickening.

Mismanagement of the war. The sorry state of our military leaders. Untrained, uneducated troops."

"There were a lot of things wrong about that war, Brad. But good and decent men and women died over there."

"At the hands of our own government."

Meg looked at him. "I can't believe that. It disgraces their memory and their sacrifice."

"You weren't there. You don't know. And you don't know what it was like to come back. To be spit on. To be a leper for doing your duty. I couldn't find a fucking job for three years!" Brad nervously passed his gun from one hand to the other. "It was Gordon Meyers who finally helped me. He told me about the MSF. About my father. We put the MSF back together — to make sure another Vietnam never happened."

Meg turned back to the steering wheel. "So what do you need my family's money for? You must be making a tidy sum trading weapons and selling drugs, however you manage to rationalize it."

"I owe some people." Brad laughed. "Too many trips to Monte Carlo. Got a little fond of the roulette wheel. Unfortunately, I lost someone else's money." The gun was waved in front of Meg's face. "You should never've hired that investigator. She stirred up a lot of trouble."

"I'm glad."

Brad grabbed her arm, twisting it until she cried out. He threw her roughly back to the wheel. "Glad? You better hope that bitch doesn't cause any more trouble."

Gripping the wheel, Meg tried to hold herself together. This guy was nuts. Crazy enough to kill

Hollis, to kill her. *No.* Steer, steer, she told herself. Think of some way out.

"Where're we going, anyway?" she asked, her voice cracking. "I'm just following the coastline." It was an aimless route.

"To South Beach Lighthouse. Meeting some friends there."

"Gregory and Meyers?"

"Uh huh."

"Then what?"

"You sign the papers. After that I'll let you know."

Meg fought to keep from throwing up. Keep him talking, she thought. At least keep him talking. "Did Meyers have anything to do with my parents' accident?" When he turned away, she said, "What the hell difference does it make now, Brad? Tell me."

"Yes. He drove them off the road."

"Why?"

The veins in Brad's neck bulged. "Because your father was a fucking traitor! A man without honor, who turned in his own comrades."

"And my mother? How do you explain her away?"

The reply was cold, chilling. "I don't. She was in the wrong place at the wrong time. These things happen in warfare."

"And what about that creep who attacked me on the boat? Was I supposed to be another victim of warfare?"

He chuckled. "Sorry, Meg. That got a little out of hand. After I heard Matty was drunk when he left for your boat, I got nervous. He has a bad temper when he drinks, but he's a good soldier." Brad clicked open the revolver's chamber, spun it and

187

snapped it shut again. "So I played the knight in shining armor. After all, I still needed you in one piece."

Meg let go of the wheel, ran to the side of the boat and was sick. Her head spun with revulsion. She wished she were dead.

Ten minutes later the lighthouse was in sight. Almost like a robot Meg steered the *Emily* toward land, using the lighthouse point as a guide. "I'll have to stay about a quarter-mile out," she said stiffly. "There's a sand bar that runs along here — not to mention the reef."

"Fine," Brad said, showing little emotion of his own. "Hope you don't mind if I borrow the rubber raft." He smiled. "Need to pick up my friends."

Meg sneered. "Some friends."

The boat was anchored. Brad inflated the raft and secured it to the starboard rail. "Sorry, Meg. But I'll have to lock you in the cabin with Hollis."

Meg heard the cabin door click shut, the lock turn.

Hollis got up from the sofa, her face red with anger. "What the hell's goin' on?"

The rage, the hurt, spilled from her. "Brad's been behind everything. He and Meyers hatched this whole plot to get my grandfather's money for gun smuggling and illegal drug sales."

Hollis shook her head. "I don't believe it."

Meg grabbed her in a bear hug. "He thinks he's

some kind of freedom fighter. Re-formed this Massachusetts Special Forces to stop the Federal government from . . . oh, I don't know from what. He's loony."

"Now what?"

"We're going to get out of here. Once Brad gets back with Meyers and Gregory and I sign those papers, our lives won't be worth shit. They'll kill us and throw us to the fish."

Hollis shoved her fists into her pockets. "You really think Brad would do that to you?"

"Hol, I don't know that man anymore. That guy's an egotistical, self-centered lost boy who's on a crash course out of control. Our only concern now is us and getting out of this mess."

"Don't forget, we're locked in." Hollis pointed toward the door. "Trapped."

"He may be a self-styled smuggling czar and, in his own head, king of Massachusetts — but the brightness from his own brilliance has temporarily blinded him. Never took time to consider that there's probably more than one set of keys to this boat. Asshole." Meg walked into the galley, rummaged through the top cupboard and snatched an extra set of keys from the upper shelf. "Here's the other set. We're no longer locked in."

"Where're we goin'?"

"First, I'm going to disable the boat so they can't start it. See if they can get to South America — or wherever it is they're going — on a rubber raft. Then you and I are going for a swim."

"To shore? That doesn't sound too smart."

"We're not going to shore. But once we get to the edge of the reef, you've got to trust me, Hol. Hang on to me and don't let go, no matter what."

"I don't like the sound of this. My swimmin's not all that great."

"We'll be okay."

Under the water, in the murky blackness along the reef, Meg clung to Hollis, their arms linked tightly. Feeling her way along the rocky underwater cliff, Meg prayed she'd remember — remember where the face of the cliff inched inward toward the caves that lay underneath the rise of rock. As she swam along the black precipice, she began to panic. The opening was gone. Should've reached it by now, she thought, should've started the climb upward. Precious seconds passed. Still holding onto Hollis, Meg frantically searched. Eternal seconds. Trying to find her way out of darkness.

Suddenly, Hollis reached from behind, grabbed Meg's shoulder and went limp. Pulling Hollis with her, Meg felt the rock-wall with her hand. With seconds of air left, she pushed ahead, feeling one last time for the crevice. Suddenly, the rocky surface was gone. She fell inward, following the swell of water upward into the rocky tunnel.

Laboring with Hollis in her arms, Meg slipped out of darkness. She gasped for air, holding Hollis's head above the surging water. She wasn't breathing. Slipping, falling, struggling with the unconscious woman's weight, Meg pulled the limp body up the rocky pathway. She laid Hollis gently on the cold stone floor and began to breathe air into her lungs, compressing life into a heart that no longer beat. Nothing.

"Goddamnit, Hollis! You're not going to leave me too!" Breathing. Compressing. Nothing. "Hollis, please!" Breathing. Compressing. Nothing. "God, please don't do this to me. I love this woman. Help me!" Meg's hands were shaking uncontrollably. She felt no strength in her arms.

"I'll help you."

It was Susan. Meg moved aside as Susan knelt down and began immediately working over Hollis, breathing air through the still lips. Meg heard a gurgling sound, then saw the movement of Hollis's eyelids. She was breathing again — coughing up water.

Susan took Hollis by the shoulders. "Let's get her inside the cave. We've got to keep her warm."

Once inside, Susan wrapped her in several blankets. A few minutes later, she was fully conscious.

"Christ, Meg. Next time you wanna go swimmin', invite someone else, okay?" Hollis said, wheezing. "I thought you'd lost your mind. Then I passed out and lost mine."

"Sorry, Hol." Meg kissed her cheek. "I'll make it up to you."

"Case of beer a month for the rest of my life. That oughta do it. And you can take over my mail route too."

Susan helped her sip some hot coffee. "Meg knew what she was doing. Thank God she didn't panic."

"Oh, I was panicked. Another few seconds —" Meg stopped.

Susan got up, turning toward the opening to the southern tunnel. Footsteps could be heard echoing from the dark pathway. Susan drew her gun. A few moments later a man emerged from the shadows. Susan smiled faintly and holstered her weapon. "Jim. Everything okay?"

"Yes. If you hurry you can still catch the action." He looked at Hollis with concern. "What happened?"

"She'll be fine. But, if you wouldn't mind contacting your people by radio, Jim, I think Miss Shea should be taken to the hospital as soon as possible." Susan looked at Meg. "Just a precaution."

Meg nodded, her hand resting in Hollis's. "Yes, I agree."

Jim's radio hissed and crackled. "Don't worry, Sue. Your friend's in good hands."

"I know."

"Oh, hell, I'm all right. Never felt better." Hollis started to cough.

"Yeah, sure," Meg said. "Don't argue. You're going."

Hollis smiled weakly. "Okay, okay. I'll be good."

Susan knelt over her. "You do look better. Your color's back. But we have to make sure. Jim's an FBI agent, so try to behave."

"FBI? Thanks a lot, Susan. I'll remember this."

"No doubt. Meg and I've got an appointment to keep. We'll see you later, okay?"

Hollis frowned. "I gotta feelin' I'm missin' all the fun. Damn, my luck!"

Meg hesitated, not really wanting to leave Hollis.

Hollis waved her away. "Get goin'. I'm fine. Really."

* * * * *

Meg and Susan followed the tunnel that led from the south side of the main cave. The tunnel twisted and turned at a gradual downward slope far beneath the cliff. The path was lighted by a burning torch Susan held aloft. Throughout the tunnel the firelight cast an eerie glow along the black-rock walls. The shadows of the two women were lost on a coal-black surface worn smooth with the ages.

Eventually the tunnel reached a sharp left turn. In front of them were a set of stairs hammered into stone by human hands. The steps rose steeply to a heavy wooden door. The door creaked inward toward darkness.

Meg followed Susan, fascinated by the maze of tunnel that had led them to a door beneath the earth. Susan's flashlight illuminated the area beyond the door, and they appeared to be in the basement of a building. Another set of stairs went up into the light.

"Susan, where are we?" Meg asked as they climbed the last stairway.

"You'll see."

At the top of the steps Meg knew. The light was sunlight. The room they entered was the ground floor of the lighthouse. "I never knew these caves existed. Beneath the cliffs — beneath the lighthouse."

Susan looked lovingly around the room. "My grandfather was the lighthouse keeper for fifty years. The state owns the building now. Once it's renovated it'll be on the state registry as an official historic site."

"That's great to hear."

"Want to head upstairs? As Jim said, the action's underway."

"Action?"

Susan held out her hand. "Come see."

They climbed the long circular flight of stairs into the glass-encased dome. The view from the top was spectacular — the ocean an endless pattern of blue. To the west high rocky cliffs dropped sharply to the beach where underwater reefs held earth from ocean.

Susan pulled Meg toward the telescope, adjusting its position slightly. Peering through it, she said, "Ah, yes. Some folks you know. Have a look."

Meg placed her right eye against the eyepiece. Instantly the vast ocean before her shrank into a tiny strip of beach. She worked to assimilate the scene. Several Coast Guard cutters hovered near the *Emily*, which was still anchored where Meg had left it. Along the shoreline Coast Guard officials, the local police and FBI agents were escorting several men into custody, including Michael Gregory, Gordon Meyers and Brad Hanson. Hand-cuffed, they were being taken aboard small motorcraft that would speed them to the cutters and away to jail. Meg stepped back from the telescope. "That's a satisfying view."

"Luis Raphael's also been taken into custody at his house on Martha's Vineyard."

"Seems you've tied up all the loose ends."

"Just about. I contacted the FBI as soon as I developed these. The proof we needed to put the whole bunch away for a long time." Susan laid the 8x10 photos on a nearby table. "Brad Hanson and Gordon Meyers at Raphael's warehouse in Boston. Took them the night I found the rifles and drugs.

The FBI seized all the contraband about an hour ago."

"Who is Michael Gregory?"

"His real name's Robert Pollard. One of Hanson's Special Forces buddies."

"Did the FBI know about the resurgence of the MSF?"

"Not until I sent that patch to Jim. The FBI knew a lot of drugs were flowing from the islands into Boston. They just weren't able to pinpoint the source until now."

Meg turned away, crossing to the other side of the large-domed room. Suddenly it was a window to her world — a world that had drastically changed. "I owe you so much." She retraced her steps. She'd managed to redefine her life, with Susan's help, into a new set of memories, without blanks and missing pieces, without secrets or deception. "You've given me a new life. Maybe not an easier one, but a more enlightened one."

"I'm sorry about Brad."

Fighting for composure, Meg looked out over the water toward the reef where her life had suddenly come full-circle. From the terrible loss of her young friend along the cliff-rock to her own irreversibly widened vision, she'd finally come to view her life without vulnerability. The new picture was startling. The loss of Kit, the loss of Brad were wounds that would be long in healing. "It's shocking when you're sure you know someone," Meg said, thinking aloud. "Then you find out it's never really possible to know anyone. Family. Lovers. Friends."

"We've got a lifetime to know each other."

"Do we?"

"Yes. And you've got Hollis too. She loves you very much. No one could ask for a better friend."

"Can we go see her?"

"You bet."

"You know, Hollis said she finally met the woman of her dreams the other night."

"Hollis said that? Yeah, right."

"No, really. I think she was serious."

Susan grabbed Meg by the waist. "Well, if Hollis has met the woman of her dreams, then she and I've got a lot more in common than I thought."

"Then we all do."

Hollis was sitting up in bed, wide-eyed and grinning. "They're makin' me breathe into this machine, Meg. It measures your lung capacity."

"Have you busted it yet?"

"Very funny," came the hoarse reply.

Susan stood uncomfortably in the doorway. "Glad to see you're feeling better, Hollis."

"Thanks, Susan. Hey, I hear you gave me mouth-to-mouth. Wish you'd waited till I was awake. I would've enjoyed it a lot more."

"Hollis, you're so bad — it's hopeless." Susan grinned. "Meg tells me you've got a new girlfriend."

Hollis crossed her arms. "Yep. This is it. I'm in love." There was a soft knock on the door. Susan stepped aside. "Hey, here she is now. Guys, meet Sherry Brent."

In strode one of the most beautiful women Meg had ever seen. She was tall, with long legs and silky auburn hair that flowed to the middle of her back.

She flashed a Lauren Hutton smile, a slight gap in her front teeth the only noticeable imperfection. She wore white shorts that revealed most of her tanned thighs, and a mint-green sleeveless blouse cut low flattered the deep curves to her breasts. Sherry shook their hands then ran to Hollis.

Susan looked at Meg and raised her eyebrows.

Lovingly, Sherry touched Hollis's face. "You okay? I got here as fast as I could, sweetie."

Hollis patted her hand. "I'm fine, honey. Nothin' to worry about."

"Well, I'm not leaving until you're better. Then I'm taking you home where I can pamper you back to health."

Susan cleared her throat. "Guess we better let these two lovebirds talk, Meg. Besides, I'm starved."

Hollis's eyes softened. "Hey, Susan. Thanks again. For saving my life, I mean. And for helping Meg."

"My pleasure."

"You take good care of her. She's the best."

Susan nodded. "I know. I finally got lucky again. Seems you did too."

Meg said good-bye to Sherry then leaned over and kissed Hollis's forehead. The sparkle from her friend's eyes settled over her heart where, finally, there was no more darkness. "When you're feeling like your old self again we'll all have dinner and celebrate."

"You bet, Meg."

"And you better get your ass out of bed soon and back to work — 'cause you know what they say, Hol."

Hollis wheezed and sputtered the words. "Yeah, yeah. I know. The damned mail must go through."

A few of the publications of
THE NAIAD PRESS, INC.
P.O. Box 10543 • Tallahassee, Florida 32302
Phone (904) 539-5965
Toll-Free Order Number: 1-800-533-1973
Mail orders welcome. Please include 15% postage.

THE COLOR OF WINTER by Lisa Shapiro. 208 pp. Romantic
love beyond your wildest dreams.   ISBN 1-56280-116-3 $10.95

FAMILY SECRETS by Laura DeHart Young. 208 pp. Enthralling
romance and suspense.   ISBN 1-56280-119-8   10.95

INLAND PASSAGE by Jane Rule. 288 pp. Tales exploring conven-
tional & unconventional relationships.   ISBN 0-930044-56-8   10.95

DOUBLE BLUFF by Claire McNab. 208 pp. 7th Detective Carol
Ashton Mystery.   ISBN 1-56280-096-5   10.95

BAR GIRLS by Lauran Hoffman. 176 pp. See the movie, read
the book!   ISBN 1-56280-115-5   10.95

THE FIRST TIME EVER edited by Barbara Grier & Christine
Cassidy. 272 pp. Love stories by Naiad Press authors.
                                           ISBN 1-56280-086-8   14.95

MISS PETTIBONE AND MISS McGRAW by Brenda Weathers.
208 pp. A charming ghostly love story.   ISBN 1-56280-151-1   10.95

CHANGES by Jackie Calhoun. 208 pp. Involved romance and
relationships.   ISBN 1-56280-083-3   10.95

FAIR PLAY by Rose Beecham. 256 pp. 3rd Amanda Valentine
Mystery.   ISBN 1-56280-081-7   10.95

PAXTON COURT by Diane Salvatore. 256 pp. Erotic and wickedly
funny contemporary tale about the business of learning to live
together.   ISBN 1-56280-109-0   21.95

PAYBACK by Celia Cohen. 176 pp. A gripping thriller of romance,
revenge and betrayal.   ISBN 1-56280-084-1   10.95

THE BEACH AFFAIR by Barbara Johnson. 224 pp. Sizzling
summer romance/mystery/intrigue.   ISBN 1-56280-090-6   10.95

GETTING THERE by Robbi Sommers. 192 pp. Nobody does it
like Robbi!   ISBN 1-56280-099-X   10.95

FINAL CUT by Lisa Haddock. 208 pp. 2nd Carmen Ramirez
Mystery.   ISBN 1-56280-088-4   10.95

FLASHPOINT by Katherine V. Forrest. 256 pp. A Lesbian
blockbuster!   ISBN 1-56280-079-5   10.95

CLAIRE OF THE MOON by Nicole Conn. Audio Book —Read
by Marianne Hyatt.   ISBN 1-56280-113-9   16.95

FOR LOVE AND FOR LIFE: INTIMATE PORTRAITS OF
LESBIAN COUPLES by Susan Johnson. 224 pp.
                                      ISBN 1-56280-091-4   14.95

DEVOTION by Mindy Kaplan. 192 pp. See the movie — read
the book!   ISBN 1-56280-093-0   10.95

SOMEONE TO WATCH by Jaye Maiman. 272 pp. 4th Robin
Miller Mystery.   ISBN 1-56280-095-7   10.95

GREENER THAN GRASS by Jennifer Fulton. 208 pp. A young
woman — a stranger in her bed.   ISBN 1-56280-092-2   10.95

TRAVELS WITH DIANA HUNTER by Regine Sands. Erotic
lesbian romp. Audio Book (2 cassettes)   ISBN 1-56280-107-4   16.95

CABIN FEVER by Carol Schmidt. 256 pp. Sizzling suspense
and passion.   ISBN 1-56280-089-1   10.95

THERE WILL BE NO GOODBYES by Laura DeHart Young. 192
pp. Romantic love, strength, and friendship.   ISBN 1-56280-103-1   10.95

FAULTLINE by Sheila Ortiz Taylor. 144 pp. Joyous comic
lesbian novel.   ISBN 1-56280-108-2   9.95

OPEN HOUSE by Pat Welch. 176 pp. 4th Helen Black Mystery.
                                      ISBN 1-56280-102-3   10.95

ONCE MORE WITH FEELING by Peggy J. Herring. 240 pp.
Lighthearted, loving romantic adventure.   ISBN 1-56280-089-2   10.95

FOREVER by Evelyn Kennedy. 224 pp. Passionate romance — love
overcoming all obstacles.   ISBN 1-56280-094-9   10.95

WHISPERS by Kris Bruyer. 176 pp. Romantic ghost story
                                      ISBN 1-56280-082-5   10.95

NIGHT SONGS by Penny Mickelbury. 224 pp. 2nd Gianna Maglione
Mystery.   ISBN 1-56280-097-3   10.95

GETTING TO THE POINT by Teresa Stores. 256 pp. Classic
southern Lesbian novel.   ISBN 1-56280-100-7   10.95

PAINTED MOON by Karin Kallmaker. 224 pp. Delicious
Kallmaker romance.   ISBN 1-56280-075-2   10.95

THE MYSTERIOUS NAIAD edited by Katherine V. Forrest &
Barbara Grier. 320 pp. Love stories by Naiad Press authors.
                                      ISBN 1-56280-074-4   14.95

DAUGHTERS OF A CORAL DAWN by Katherine V. Forrest.
240 pp. Tenth Anniversay Edition.   ISBN 1-56280-104-X   10.95

BODY GUARD by Claire McNab. 208 pp. 6th Carol Ashton
Mystery.   ISBN 1-56280-073-6   10.95

CACTUS LOVE by Lee Lynch. 192 pp. Stories by the beloved
storyteller.   ISBN 1-56280-071-X   9.95

SECOND GUESS by Rose Beecham. 216 pp. 2nd Amanda Valentine
Mystery.   ISBN 1-56280-069-8   9.95

THE SURE THING by Melissa Hartman. 208 pp. L.A. earthquake
romance.   ISBN 1-56280-078-7   9.95

A RAGE OF MAIDENS by Lauren Wright Douglas. 240 pp. 6th Caitlin
Reece Mystery.   ISBN 1-56280-068-X   10.95

TRIPLE EXPOSURE by Jackie Calhoun. 224 pp. Romantic drama
involving many characters.   ISBN 1-56280-067-1   9.95

UP, UP AND AWAY by Catherine Ennis. 192 pp. Delightful
romance.   ISBN 1-56280-065-5   9.95

PERSONAL ADS by Robbi Sommers. 176 pp. Sizzling short
stories.   ISBN 1-56280-059-0   9.95

FLASHPOINT by Katherine V. Forrest. 256 pp. Lesbian
blockbuster!   ISBN 1-56280-043-4   22.95

CROSSWORDS by Penny Sumner. 256 pp. 2nd Victoria Cross
Mystery.   ISBN 1-56280-064-7   9.95

SWEET CHERRY WINE by Carol Schmidt. 224 pp. A novel of
suspense.   ISBN 1-56280-063-9   9.95

CERTAIN SMILES by Dorothy Tell. 160 pp. Erotic short stories.
                                             ISBN 1-56280-066-3   9.95

EDITED OUT by Lisa Haddock. 224 pp. 1st Carmen Ramirez
Mystery.   ISBN 1-56280-077-9   9.95

WEDNESDAY NIGHTS by Camarin Grae. 288 pp. Sexy
adventure.   ISBN 1-56280-060-4   10.95

SMOKEY O by Celia Cohen. 176 pp. Relationships on the
playing field.   ISBN 1-56280-057-4   9.95

KATHLEEN O'DONALD by Penny Hayes. 256 pp. Rose and
Kathleen find each other and employment in 1909 NYC.
                                             ISBN 1-56280-070-1   9.95

STAYING HOME by Elisabeth Nonas. 256 pp. Molly and Alix
want a baby . . . or do they?   ISBN 1-56280-076-0   10.95

TRUE LOVE by Jennifer Fulton. 240 pp. Six lesbians searching
for love in all the "right" places.   ISBN 1-56280-035-3   10.95

GARDENIAS WHERE THERE ARE NONE by Molleen Zanger.
176 pp. Why is Melanie inextricably drawn to the old house?
                                             ISBN 1-56280-056-6   9.95

These are just a few of the many Naiad Press titles — we are the oldest and
largest lesbian/feminist publishing company in the world. Please request a
complete catalog. We offer personal service; we encourage and welcome
direct mail orders from individuals who have limited access to bookstores
carrying our publications.